Souled To Death

By: *Kyla M. Wassil*

Being a biker is not a hobby, it's a lifestyle.

𝔄 word from the author

I have been on two wheels since I was nineteen years old and it has changed my life immensely. I live to ride, rain or shine, no matter the temperature. A lot of people may have a negative opinion about motorcyclists, but we are all the same; we're all people.

I thank my brothers and sisters who ride just the same. I send love and prayers out to those who have lost someone in an accident. I have been in a few myself, but my driven passion keeps me on the horse.

We all have one thing in common, no matter our colors, no matter our purpose or leisure and that's the two wheels that we ride on.

For those who drive motorcycles or the likes, ride safe and ride your fucking hearts out!

Thank you.

One

Have you ever looked at a magazine more than once, hoping to see something different? That's kind of how I look at life, even the people who are involved in my little conservative world, no matter how inept others may seem. We tend to overlook the simplest of things. We may recognize, but never truly see everything. If we are so equipped on judging upon a first glance, you can almost bet that we are missing the bigger picture.

I have passed a great deal of faces in my life, shook many hands and walked across various planes of foreign soil. There are things even I am guilty of never questioning. If we don't understand something, we choose to create a crude opinion on what we believe, maybe even what we've been told once before. We allow social media the advantage to shape and mold our opinions solely based upon 'their conclusions'.

The free will of man that was frowned upon has made all seem arrogant. Even one's pride has been taken advantage of overtime and without knowledge of the existence of others, or evidence given to pen upon paper, or a sight captured through a lens, we will always wonder. Without wonder, the unknown would cease to exist and without the unknown…who will then adapt and discover?

*S*taring out the window as the continuous trance of trees flew by nearly put me to sleep. A smile soon stretched across my face when my eyes landed upon *Tennessee Welcomes You.* I was finally home and couldn't wait to pull the only woman who has never left me, nor broken my heart tightly into my embrace. I haven't seen these blue skies in months and to breathe in the scent of Iris was the valued proof that my birthplace was happy to have me back.

My beautiful mother awaited me as the bus came to a stop. Age never seemed to wear on her until recently, though her vibrant smile has always been my favorite aspect; humble and never changing. The smell of warm vanilla musk flowed through my nostrils as I squeezed until all breath had left her lungs.

"You look more and more like your father each year you age." She smiled warmly.

"I'm sure he'd be proud to know that his good looks were passed down."

"Oh, how I've missed you, Easton!"

"I've missed you too, ma."

A small tear rolled down her cheek as the smooth of her palm swiped the stubble of my face. It has only been three years since my father passed and no matter what, it still gets to her. Even with a perfect smile and a shaken voice, I still see the pain held prisoner in her eyes.

Pulling up to the house I grew up in had my inner child breaking free. The fenced in porch was still comforted by the colorful cultivation that is delicately nourished by the hands of wisdom. The squeak of worn springs held flush with the hinge brought back memories as the smell of southern food dug into the core of my hunger. Dinner was one of lesser words as my mother sat reticent across from me. I hated knowing she was cooped up here all alone quite often, though she claims to never mind the times of solitude; I begged to differ.

"Have you spoken to Draper, lately?"

"A little… here and there. He told me that he always comes over to see you. I think it's all due to the fact that you always cook for him."

My mother laughed innocently. *"It isn't like I have had anyone else to enjoy my cooking."*

My smile instantly fell into a frown. Though I had duty greater beyond kissing my mother goodnight each time the moon rose, I still felt guilty having not been around like I should have. Especially after suffering such a great loss.

"Stop forking at your taters and go give him a call. He misses you like nobody's business."

"After the dishes." I grabbed up my plate.

As I turned on the faucet to begin cleaning up, headlights pulled into the driveway. I recognized the car almost immediately.

"No need to make that call…he's already here."

I ran out the front door with my heart anxious beneath my chest. His hair was longer than usual, but it suited him just fine.

Shaking it to view me clearly, Draper opened his arms wider than the horizon. *"It's about damn time you brought your ass home! It's so good to see you again."*

Saving the whole catching up spiel, we decided to hit a local tavern five miles out to grab some drinks for the occasion. The town was louder than I had anticipated as we walked through the entrance. I never fancied getting trashed at local biker bars, but when that's all you've got, you generally take advantage. Leaned up against the bar waiting to be served, a sweet southern voice broke my attention.

"Well, I'll be damned! I never thought you'd set foot back in this place."

I glanced over to see a girl I had graduated with. Her eyes locked on mine as she slightly bit her bottom lip with allurement.

"It has been said, but I came back. My ma needs me…ya know the reason why, I'm sure." I cleared my throat.

"What can I get you two…fine, young gentlemen?" She winked.

"Just a beer for now."

For about an hour, Draper and I sat at the bar conversing about past times with Miley, slowly enduring the pain settling in my ass as it began to go numb. The sound of a rugged disagreement stirred up behind us. I immediately directed my attention to see a group of bikers hassling another gentleman by the jukebox. The nerve of honor that pricked in my gut had me watch rather closely. A man of ebony descent was the victim of what was itching to turn into an old fashioned white supremacist ass beating.

I took a long sip from my bottle trying my best to neglect the ignorance of malice behavior in its purest development. Seeing the fear caught up in Miley's eyes had me more alert of the situation's severity. Once more bikers began jumping in practically defeating the man who stood a lone wolf had me fly from my barstool. Draper was soon to follow my lead, knowing my instinct to intervene when I should have left it alone.

At the time, I had no idea what I was up against. I have been carefully trained to take precaution, to be observant, but watching wasn't bringing justice. The rush of impulsion landed my hand on the attackers shoulder, swinging him around to face me. Before I could open my mouth to speak, his fist met my jaw. Instantly, I became defensive placing my hands on his leather vest to shove him towards the door. More bikers swarmed in throwing punches left and right when Draper tried his hardest to help me fend them off.

"You made a grand mistake by putting your hands on me, son."

"I don't believe that what you're doing is in any light of acceptable behavior, "son"." I jeered while thrashing my forehead into his as he teetered backwards nearly falling over.

Before I could shove him completely outside, the flick of a blade caught the glimpse of light that penetrated my eyes. I could hear people in chaotic shambles as the fight became a battle of life or death. I was told more than I'd like to keep track of on how to *never* allow another to assault you, make you feel unsafe, or use weapons against you even if it were your own.

A quick snatch to his wrist and the blade was now in my control. I didn't want to hurt anyone, but the man held a high degree of resistance. Most people would cower, maybe even have stayed put to begin with. But, I am not the average Joe…my instinct is to protect and that is what I was doing. Protecting my life and those around me, defending what was right.

His eyes widened as I shoved the blade deep into his lower abdomen. My jaw fell open just as his did, watching him slowly lowering to the ground below.

"Call an ambulance!" Draper yelled.

Flashbacks of war approached my thought process as the familiar sight of blood ran down my hand. Was I wrong for what I did? I was only trying to save myself…to save the man who was breathing heavily against the jukebox with a busted face and bloodied teeth.

No one's life is more valuable than your own. Maybe I needed to stop believing that, only because I have been placed in dangerous situations for the last eight years. I have seen and done things I cannot take back. I have seen more than one person take their last breath in my wake. But I was forced to drag my boots through the reddened dirt and swallow the unfavorable taste of dry desert and destruction down my throat.

I never stop thinking about the families I have destroyed, the lives of sons and daughters that I have taken. Battle is more than running around with a rifle and a painted face…it's the warrior's purpose that life illuminates. One of the most crucial and unforgiving things to have to challenge and accept is looking into the eyes of your enemy and having not known their name. I have a heart full of honor and a mind of integrity, but scars run deeper than the scratches on my armor. Nobody here knew death better than me…or so I thought.

Red and blue lights flashed in the darkness of the atmosphere. Officers ran through the entrance clearing the bar, asking questions and taking statements. I, of course had to give mine, but watching the paramedics strap my victim to a gurney made my stomach twist in knots. The others who were with him had fled before authority showed up. As much as I wanted to forget about what happened, I couldn't. It was just like every other time I had to watch someone be in critical pain, much worse by my own hand.

I raised my balled up fist, staring the officer dead in the eye as I opened it to reveal the knife that claimed my fingerprints. He placed it into an evidence bag before resting a hand of silent reassurance upon my shoulder. *"Thank you for your honesty and also a big thank you for your service, Mr. Ruckett."* He took note of my military I.D.

In the distance, I could see Draper rested on a barstool icing his wounds while talking with another officer. I thought I had come home to find peace, to free my mind and soul from guilt and violence. Yet, I found myself feeling the same damn way I always had; *alone.*

The ride home was one of loud silence. I don't believe I have ever seen Draper so scared in all my years of knowing him. I guess that's why he allowed me to leave this town and fight for the nation's mistakes while he stayed home in a warm bed.

"Are you gonna be okay?"

"I think I should be the one asking you that…"

I ran a hand aggressively through the tiny hairs on my scalp. It isn't his fault that he didn't understand the way I felt. How could he know?

"Give me a call tomorrow if you need anything. It's gonna be just fine. Misunderstandings at bars happen all the time, I'm sure."

"It wasn't just a misunderstanding." I said lowly.

Draper scratched at his forehead as he took a deep breath. *"Was it scary over there?"*

"More than you could ever imagine." I sighed. *"But, you're right. It'll be okay."* I smirked with uncertainty while opening the car door.

I took a moment to enjoy the night air, reminiscing on the times Draper and I had campouts right there in the front yard. We'd stay up all night telling ghost tales and made a competition out of whose was the scariest or goriest. Hell, I'd win nowadays without a doubt; only now, mine weren't made up...they were real.

Entering the house to a still darkness, I made my way into the kitchen trying to locate the light switch. Pressing my hands against the sink, I noticed blood stained on my hand. Wanting to sever it off completely, I took a brillo pad to the area taking a layer of skin along with it. I was frustrated, momentarily losing my self-control. A ferocious slug to the air had the silver meshy ball slam against the wall. I eased myself with a deep breath not wanting to wake my mother. Lord knows she didn't need to begin asking questions before the sun rose.

Two

Rested on the porch rocking back and forth in my chair, a light breeze sent wispy chills across my bare feet naturally causing me to tuck them beneath the afghan my mother had made me when I was younger.

I pulled the cup of warm tea to my face letting the steam tickle my nostrils. My mother was seated in a wicker chair beside me, glancing at a newspaper.

I drew in a deep breath focusing my gaze upon her furrowed expression. Without meeting my eyes, she acknowledged the fact I had been staring, maybe she even felt my wonder radiating through my annoying sigh.

"What is it, son?"

"Why you always reading those damn things? They never tell you anything good."

"Well, for one, I am doing a crossword puzzle. And two, it relaxes me. I like to know what's going on with the world. You should try it."

I tilted my head to the side with a smirk from her knowing my reason for not. *"Why you all the sudden interested in crosswords?"*

"Doctor says it's good for the memory, keeps your brain working. I also do word searches from time to time. Why, you got a comment for that, too?"

I chuckled as she raised her eyes above the frame of her glasses. *"No ma'am. But you act as if you're gonna forget something beyond the grocery list."*

"Easton…" She became serious. *"You know it runs in our family."*

My posture slacked from being annoyed with the fact. I gripped my cup looking out into the distance not wanting to hear anymore. *"You're gonna be fine, ma."* I clenched my jaw.

I drank the last of my tea while standing to my feet to get a refill. Before I could enter the house, my mother stopped me.

"Now that you're home, what are you planning on doing? I read an article about how it can be a struggle to adjust to civilian life again. You know I do not ask you further questions, because I do not care to know. Battling possible memory loss and nightmares will be too much to juggle."

I rolled my eyes with another sigh. *"Ma, would you quit with that crap? As much as you hate talking about my previous career, the amount is well shared with knowing your medical issues!"*

She looked taken aback by my sudden change of attitude. I immediately became apologetic realizing I had just raised my voice to her. I never do that...I never disrespect her. *Ever!*

"I understand and hope that your temper is over a wounded heart over your father...but, he and I differ with as you say "medical issues", Easton. I have already begun showing signs. You just haven't been here." Her voice crackled.

It dug deep, that's all it took to twist the spear through my heart. My chest ached at the thought of something happening to the only parent I had left. It's never easy losing someone, I'd know all about that. A parent is completely different. I never thought I'd have to say goodbye to my father so soon, but a heart attack never gives you much of a notice.

"Please don't make me feel any worse than I already do. You and pa both knew I had to leave and do something with my life. What's important is that I am home now. I am not leaving you again. I promise."

"Yeah, you say that until some pretty little Dixie comes and takes you away." She joked.

"You will always come first." My voice softened.

After enjoying one last cup, I decided to busy myself with mangling beneath the hood of my father's old Bronco that had the doors taken off. I needed something to do since my mother had gone out with some of her girlfriends to play bingo. I remember taking that bad boy out to go bogging with the fellas. I even had my first duck hunting trip in that old thing. The paint was well preserved having been kept in the garage beneath a cover for a few years now.

I was in the process of changing the oil when a loud rumbling, almost as if thunder was rolling down the road sparked my curiosity. I turned my head to see as much as possible while lying beneath the truck. A group of motorcycles came pulling up in my driveway. I figured they must've made a wrong turn off the highway or were probably lost.

Inching my way out to stand to my feet, I could see them hopping of their bikes to approach me.

"Can I help you gentlemen?"

"Yeah…as a matter of fact, you can." One laughed sarcastically.

I swallowed hard while wiping my oily fingers clean with a rag. Before I could open my mouth to ask another question, I was slammed against driver's side. I threw my hands up not understanding what was going on. He pushed me into the aggressive group he showed up with, having them physically restrain me. Taking ahold of the crowbar that lied in the front seat, he took it straight to my abdomen just enough to bruise tremendously.

I instantly doubled over completely winded as my veins constricted in my head. I flinched at the sight of him raising it above my head and for a moment, I actually believed I was about to meet my demise and I couldn't help but wonder why?

"Benjamin, he wants him alive remember?"

"You're right." He spat on the ground before dropping the crowbar with a thud.

As my eyes met his, a fist drew back before knocking me straight in the nose. I blacked out before knowing what hit me. I thought I had a bad dream until I woke up in a place I had never been before. I jerked my shoulders as my chest pressed tightly into the rope that held me prisoner to a chair. My vision was blurred and all I could see were a bunch of hardcore, rough-edged men surrounding me. A slender man stepped forward with a bottle of vodka gripped in his palm.

"You have no fucking idea what the hell you've done…" He began. *"I know what's going through your mind, "why me?", "what is happening?". "What I don't quite understand is why the fuck you chose to nearly kill one of my brothers, last night."*

The reality of what I did was now serving the retaliation in the worst way possible.

"I…I had…"

"You had what? No idea? Yeah, I'm sure. You stabbed a man with his own fucking knife and now he is in the damn hospital on the verge of death. Don't you feel like a fucking hero? All you had to do was mind your business just like every other dumb fuck in this town. Who the hell are you? Better yet, who the fuck do you think you are?"

I couldn't respond fast enough before he doused my entire face with liquor. It burned the cuts in my skin and set my eyes on fire. He didn't want my explanation—he didn't care. He wanted me dead. Shoving the bottle deep into my mouth, he then yanked my head back as it aggressively poured down my throat.

I choked, I couldn't breathe—I couldn't think.

He removed the bottle, clanking it against my teeth as warm liquor shot from my nose and out of my mouth. I coughed trying to catch my breath before he reinserted the glass deep into my mouth. The bottle ground against my teeth while I tried screaming to make him stop. He just laughed, taking a hand to my throat.

"I should fucking kill you. Your life plus a thousand more wouldn't equal his."

"Then, why don't you?" My eyes narrowed.

"Good question." The back of his hand displaying steel and Emerald met my cheek. *"I don't want to just get rid of you. Your heroism could be a new human molecular advantage…if you are one instilled with obedience. My brothers informed me of what a fight you put up. Makes sense seeing as how you served two enlistments in the Corps, didn't you, Gunnery Sergeant Ruckett?"*

I clenched my jaw feeling its soreness drive deep into my skull. This man was of something serious and to know he already had personal information on me had me backed into a corner. I had to ask myself if it was really worth curling my lip up with a smartass remark. Then…my mother came to mind. And you can bet your life that I kept my fucking mouth shut.

"I'm not going to take your life and you can thank the fact that it is only because Eden is still breathing, for the time being. I will give you a deposition before the club. You can either prospect for us in which we will

know everything you do, know everywhere you go, and everything about you. Your time is our time. Or you can deny my proposal and go out with a bullet in your fucking skull. Your choice."

"And I suggest you decide rather quickly." The man earlier who was called Benjamin stepped toward me with his arms folded.

Looking through him I saw a female of petite stature hidden in the shadows of the room. Her eyes were serious, yet fearful. And for a moment, I had thought I'd seen a guardian angel or was I just being helplessly optimistic?

"I'll do it...on one condition."

"Ha. You have no fucking conditions. You belong to us now." He flicked upon a large hunting knife, placing the blades edge to my neck. *"If you believe in God, I suggest you pray and thank him for saving your life."* He moved the blade to the rope that bound me, cutting me loose. Taking both hands to my shirt pulling me to my feet, his dark eyes drilled a hole through my soul. *"I'm Ryder, your clubs president. Welcome to your new family and just know your life is about to change...forever."* He growled promisingly.

I took a broad look around the room, memorizing the faces I was now forced to see from that day forward. His irrefutable proposal tore my personal discretion to pieces. Who knew my actions would have led me to this? Maybe this was my karma from past trials I was placed in. Was God upset with me for the things that I have done? Either way, I had no unreal explanation for how my mother was going to take seeing the marks engraved on my face. Then again, I did this to myself. Did I not?

Ryder was right; my life had changed in that very moment. I just didn't know the extension at the time. Walking towards the door of the warehouse, I was uncertain on how to get home considering I was unaware of where I was to begin with. An older gentleman stood by the entrance with a very depressive look upon his face. Did he feel sorry for me? Or was he disappointed over the fact of having to look after another utterly unconcerned jackass who stumbled across his path and those of his club members? I knew nothing about these guys, their purpose or what was soon to be asked of me. Though I was quite certain I'd be learning rather soon and rather quickly.

Making my way towards the entrance, the gentleman offered to give me a ride home. I did nothing but accept his generous proposition.

I leaned back against what they called the 'sissybar', relaxing as much as possible on the ride home. Riding a bike is much different than any other motor vehicle. You feel free, nothing is closing you in, yet you're taking a chance on life without any surroundings to protect you.

A harsh gale whipped against my face and through my hair as tiny granites of sand particles nearly pierced my squinted eyes. I found myself focusing on the man's patches on the back of his vest. It had a Celtic cross with the triquetra in its center, colored in turquoise, red, and gray. An interesting Celtic design comforted that of the cross as his top patch read *Keltic Disciples* above the cross with the letter M on the left hand side and the letter C on the right hand side. The bottom patch below the cross read *East Knoxville, TN.* I had no knowledge of what any of it meant, but from the worn thread and faded colors, I assumed he had been a member for quite some time.

Pulling into my driveway, I hopped off nearly collapsing to the ground as the pain in my gut had my legs quivering. I looked the man in his eyes with a thank you before my attention fell upon the decorativeness of his front side. All of his patches were another language to me and a deep part of me wondered what meaning they held.

"Listen to me carefully as I say this. There is no halfway in, kid. You must commit if you want to live to see each day. This isn't like the military and it isn't some rundown carnival ride. It is now your life and you must conduct yourself in such a manner of constant value and respect."

"No disrespect, but I understand the value of respect."

"This is different. Your sergeant wouldn't put you in harm's way if you made a mistake. He would not place you in fatal danger and expect you to give your life."

"No...that he would not, but I'd give my life anyway for my purpose."

A spark of optimism tugged at the corners of his mouth. *"I advise you to use that to your advantage. You can call me Adam. I am the club's Secretary. I will be of any aid as much as I am allowed. You seem like a good kid. I don't want to even think about what Ryder has in store for you."*

"I appreciate any advice given."

Adam cranked his throttle with a nod before whipping around to leave. I stood stuck in place not wanting to enter my house looking the way I did. My tongue ran along the fresh cut imbedded inside my upper lip as I made my way towards the spigot located outside by the flowerbed.

Crouching down, I pressed my palm firmly against my wounded abdomen. Raising my shirt, I witnessed deep bruising setting in with the perfected shape of the crowbar. My left hand shook as I reached to turn on the water. Cupping my hand, I gently dabbed water onto my face as the liquid reddened across both hands. Severe pain stung my face as frustration drove my wet fingers through my scalp. I wanted to get a look at my own appearance before my mother had the chance to. I've never lied to her…I never lie to anyone, so what was I to say when she asked the tormenting questions of concern?

Rounding the corner to the front of the house, I quietly snuck through the porch and inside to reach the bathroom. When I looked in the mirror, I immediately panicked with horrible flashbacks from my unforgettable times in the land of unforgiving ruthlessness. I've seen my face like this on multiple occasions and it was never a pretty sight. The cut on my lip was symmetrical with the one I had received from the buttstock of a rifle years ago. The area was numb till this day when I actually paid attention to its existence.

I could hear my mother shuffling around the cabinets in the kitchen, almost in what seemed like frustration. Panic set in as I pressed my back against the door. I didn't want to face her, hell—I didn't want her to know that I was even home. I turned off the light, standing in a momentary silence. I was rather good at sneaking around, being kept hidden in plain sight. But hiding from your own mother was an entirely different challenge.

Once all sound had subsided, I crept out making my way to my bedroom. I had only hoped my mother assumed I was out somewhere with Draper, supposedly seeking a new occupation.

Three

The room was motionless as I straddled the line between stages of sleep. A gust of wind blew through the curtains, rolling across the bareness of my chest. I could sense the moon's illuminance cast a silhouette in the far corner of my room, leaving it to curiously wander. My breathing then deepened, yet my body lied stationary. A brief image of the woman I caught a peculiar glimpse of entered the lighting with daring eyes and an alluring smile. Strands of metallic radiance brazed across vitreous skin; marveling in the innocence of desire. Nearing my position to break the thin membrane of prohibited contact wired shut with reluctance had paused my breathing. A stare as cold as stone yet sharp as a knife, drew me in deeper beyond my own control.

Dense fingernails pricked the surface of my skin as a light trace of pleasant chills danced an unfamiliar sensation throughout my body. Gliding to my throat, delicate fingers soon turned into a vice grip of deadly threat…or was it one of warning? My eyes shot open, locking in on those of my new found enemy; *Ryder*.

Gasping for air, I sat upright panting for the slightest of oxygen to enter my lungs. The misery bestowed upon me was becoming a reality before I even had the chance to accept it. I was once transformed into a man of steel and honor, now I was a man sworn to ride the mechanism of modified iron while begging for his merit of distinction. It very well brought a whole new meaning to *Semper Fidelis*.

Before I could pop my freshly buttered bagel into my salivating mouth, Adam pulled into my driveway. My teeth clamped down as my fingers made a spastic attempt to finish buttoning my shirt. The echoing rumble denoted the fact he wasn't alone. Forcing the crisped yeast down my throat, I fought from choking as my irritation flung the front door wide open.

"What are you doing here so early?"

The one they referred to as 'Benjamin' hopped off his bike, rubbing his palms together in a smooth fashion. *"Didn't your mother ever teach you how impolite it is to speak with a full mouth?"* His right hand came across my cheek as blood immediately rushed to the area.

I had to take a mental break of awareness to reassess myself before things ended badly where we stood. *"Apologies..."* I snarked as chewed up particles ejected from my mouth and onto the ground.

His hand struck the other cheek causing my back teeth to clamp down forcefully onto skin. Saliva excreted around the wounded area as I drew in a deep breath with a sharpened gaze.

"And then the fucker has the nerve to fucking spit? Jesus Christ, you've got a rude awakening...nequam." He shook his head in disappointment.

"What did you just call me?"

Benjamin curled up the side of his mouth with sarcasm, directing his remark to the members who came with him. *"Abeamus!"* He grabbed ahold of his handlebars, starting up his engine.

"He said let's go…" Adam informed.

"I didn't know there was a barrier of language."

"Ha, there's a lot you are still unaware of. Get on."

I did as instructed, holding on for dear life as we flew down the highway. We pulled up to a large warehouse with the letters AOA engraved on the front above the entrance. My knees began to weaken watching dozens of other members swarm through the doorway, chit-chatting amongst one another. Men of all ages and sizes appeared before me as my heart rate accelerated with each step I made. Every member displayed the same patch Adam had on the back of his vest.

Following suit behind Adam, a hand yanked me by the back of the shirt, throwing me away from the doorway. I caught myself on one foot before completely collapsing to the dirt. Benjamin gave a dominant huff over his shoulder leaving me exactly where I had fallen. Laughing to myself in disbelief, I ran my tongue along the inside of my bottom lip accepting his challenge.

Making my way inside, a loud ding of a bell had everyone's attention as all conversation ceased. I saw Adam and Benjamin take a seat at the long round table that centered the room. Other members stood by listening or hung around the bar.

Ryder stood at the far end of the table resembling the leader's position. I assumed the most valuable members of the hierarchy sat in a specific position at the table during their meetings. I was uncertain on where to stand, so I remained hidden within the shadows while their meeting commenced.

"All right, glad everyone could make it. I need all issues brought to my attention so we can vote properly upon a solution."

The breath fell from my mouth catching sight of that divine female that rested inches away from Ryder's left-hand side. She laid a whisper into his ear as he carefully listened while tapping his fingers atop the wooden surface. I found myself dying to know just how greatly her voice would affect my ears through audible sensation.

Her lipstick brighter than any crimson I've seen paint an object and her eyes darker than any shadow slain to the mercy beneath my heel. Becoming inept as I failed to remain inconspicuous, I stepped forward accidentally crushing the toes of the man who stood nearby.

His eyes met mine as they enlarged with pain. *"Heus, perfide!"*

"I'm sorry. I did not mean to." I swallowed hard.

His hands took a hold of my shirt, running me towards the table. My feet could not slow the momentum as he flung me into the air before slamming me down against the table top.

"Oh, I forgot to mention boss. Et induxi vos aliquid…" Benjamin laughed devilishly.

Ryder abruptly stood from his chair, slamming his hands down with a loud crack. Before the man could pound his fist into my face, Ryder ordered him off.

"Mr. Ruckett…so glad you rudely decided to grace us with your presence." His voice was smooth yet unnerving.

I slid to my feet adjusting my shirt with embarrassment. What was I to say while the entire room's gaze narrowed my being into the size of a fucking dime?

"Since you're here, come stand beside me."

I was hesitant at first until a hand shoved me forward followed by the echo of over twenty grown men belting out into harsh laughter.

"Silentium!" Ryder commanded. *"How dare any of you laugh? This arrogant little prick is now every one of yours goddamn responsibility. He was pronounced our new prospect and you will treat him as such. If anyone cares to do otherwise, they can bring their concerns directly to my attention. Genus familia est…sanguinis est sanguis. Or have we all forgotten?"*

The woman who clung to Ryder's side with severity held up a leather vest with only a few patches embroidered into its dark fabric. Holding her arm out in full extension, the vest plopped down carelessly. As if it held no meaning to her…as if *I* held no meaning. Ryder snatched it up, facing its backside for everyone to view. *"This is your cut. You will wear it every time you enter this clubhouse. You will wear it on every ride. If you fail to remember, consequences shall follow. Think of it as a permanent part of your everyday attire from now on. Also, these patches on the back are your rockers. The top one is your club's name which we are the Keltic Disciples. Your patch is our "probationary" patch, in time if the entire club agrees upon a traditional vote, will you then be eligible to display and represent our name. The bottom rocker is your chapter which is East Knoxville, Tennessee. You must earn your center patch, your 1%er patch, as well as the right to wear the initials M.C. for "motorcycle club". Remember, this cut does not under any circumstance, belong to you. It is club property. If you fail to abide by any bylaws in which are verbally read to you or advanced legibly, you will be dealt with accordingly. Understood?"*

For a moment, I had no idea on how to properly respond. I was about to be officially branded the bitch of a motorcycle gang, one in which did not take too lightly on arrogance nor ignorance. Not even the simplicity of pardon in regards of honestly forgetting to wear my fucking vest in which labeled me as such.

"Loqui, pugnas!" Benjamin bit out.

I couldn't understand his Latin tongue, but by the harshness of his tone I knew it meant I should answer.

"Yes, all is clearly understood."

"Excellent. Now put the damn thing on instead of standing there looking fucking foolish."

I slid it on one arm at a time. It fit snugly to my torso as I smoothed my hands down the thick leather.

"The patch that reads "prospect" is your identification or "call-sign". If and when in the future you gain a nickname or position, it shall then replace it. Anytime you introduce yourself, you will refer to yourself as "prospect, Easton", nothing else! If any full patched member is to ask something of you, you had better fucking do it. No questions asked!"

"I think nequam suits him quite well, boss." Benjamin snickered.

"Obseres palatum!" Ryder barked.

My eyes met those of the captivating woman whose perfume soaked into the fibers that clutched my body. An innocent smile pulled back the corners of her mouth at the sound of Ryder's authoritative remark. My gaze intensified on her every move; though her eyes never dared reaching mine or anywhere remotely within the proximity in which I stood. She looked much younger than Ryder; the tightness of her flawless skin bared no lifelong wrinkles or scars, but her eyes told another story—one that concealed suppressed history. Maybe that's where her scars lied…beneath the surface like most people.

"Another thing you should be well aware of is if we call you…you had better drop whatever the fuck it is you find more important and come running. Nothing or no one is more important than this club. You must prove to us that you deserve to be here, that you want to be here. If you fail to comply or show up, you will be dealt with

and trust me when I say you don't want us to come find you. You better turn your mindset into the fact you truly want to be here...I don't mind making you feel right at home." Ryder's eyes narrowed.

I could feel my chest bow inward from the lack of breathing. *"Got it."*

"How can you sit there and allow him to spat such disrespect towards you, boss? He sure as hell doesn't deserve to be here despite the fact of his hand being forced."

"Benjamin, that is for me to fucking decide."

Within seconds, he and Benjamin entered an outlandish feud in Latin that lasted several minutes. I swallowed hard trying to pick up on a possible interpretation through their emotions and hand gestures. It was all but possible when I claimed little knowledge from history class, but never cared to store away the language's origin nor cared to speak a lick a day in my life.

"I feel disrespected that you even have the nerve to question my fucking position of authority. You would choose now to show your ass, wouldn't you?" Ryder's hand gripped around the back of my neck with a menace squeeze.

I felt my lungs freeze as excitement rose inside the fiery pits of Benjamin's hollow eyes. My body remained tense beneath the hand of my new found 'Dominus', as his fingers applied more pressure. The wince in my expression put worry in the eyes of our audience as they all stood in silence.

"Satis fratres. I do believe there is more important business to conduct. We still have yet to discuss our funds with Quaestor." Adam interrupted.

"Why don't you put your new little pet to work while we finish our meeting, Ryder?" Quaestor remarked. *"All in favor, say I."*

The club repeated only to singe the aggression, melting the scorn from his face.
Ryder demanded Benjamin to show me behind the bar and give formal, yet plausible instruction on what it was that I was now responsible for doing. With a snarl, he obeyed while motioning for me to follow suit.

Rounding the corner of the bar, Benjamin slid a few shot glasses my way along with a rag. *"When your ass is behind our bar, you treat each object you touch as if it were your own. You break anything and I'll break a bone in your fragile body. If no one is up here requesting drinks, you are to be cleaning the glassware until spotless. Every tap should be free from clogging and mold, and all alcohol bottles are to be stocked and plentiful, understood?"*

"Yes..." I glared.

Benjamin sensed my negativity as his eyes locked in. Lurching forward he pulled my forehead to his, holding me tightly in place. *"Look here you arrogant little bastard. I get that you don't want to be here, but you did this to yourself. You belong to us, remember that! You can either make this as less in difficulty as possible or you can keep digging your own grave. I don't give a fuck, as long as you reframe from dragging my ass down with you. You will do as you are told or you will die!"*

Throwing my head back unregulated my balance as I toppled over knocking a glass to the floor. A sigh of irritation escaped my lips when it shouldn't have. Ready to receive another palm collision to my cheek, Benjamin stood collected while glancing down at the broken shards. *"Well, aren't you going to clean that up?"*

Without hesitation, I bent over gathering up the broken pieces merely grimacing as tiny fragments pierced my fingertips. Suddenly, I left red droplets trickling onto the floor and that of the bar's surface. While running my cuts beneath warm water, a shadow closed in on me causing my eyes to rise. Landing on Ryder's prized possession, my heart nearly stopped.

"You'd better get a move on with learning much quicker."

"Why do you say that?" My brow twitched.

"It's just an intelligent, yet obvious suggestion." She arched a brow above her shades. *"Two Yuengling's, please?"*

I slid open the cooler door pulling out the desired brewery. Popping the tops with intentional lag, I watched another raise of her brow radiate impatience. A playful smile raised my cheeks, but she didn't return the favor. Sliding the bottles in her direction, I kept my hands firmly gripped around their necks.

"You play a rather dangerous game, Mr. Ruckett. One in which you will surly lose. I strongly

advise you keep your eyes forward and your mind free
from any conjuring thoughts of me." Jerking the bottles
into her possession, she walked away with nothing short
of confidence.

I wasn't sure by what she meant, but I knew
for certain that I was not playing any games. I wanted
her just as a puppy wanted more than a lick of a milk
bone. I wanted to gnaw her to pieces, relishing in the
desirable taste of forbidden fruit that taunted me into
the absence of my mind.

Lucky me for having the pleasure of staying
late just to ensure every God damn glass was spotless to
their satisfaction.

Throughout the night, I continued to
absentmindedly watch her every movement as the
tempest slowly drew me in with lustrous affliction. How
'dangerous' could she *really* be?

Adam took the continuous liberty of hauling
my ass to and from the clubhouse when necessary. I got
the feeling he would be one of the few who didn't want
to publically disembowel me and leave me to the
Vulchers. The only diseased carnivore I was up against
around here was Benjamin. Then again, doesn't every
group have their inconsequential asshole?

I stretched my legs after sliding off the back of
Adam's bike. He pressed his lips together in deep
thought before releasing a sigh.

"What is it?" I became concerned.

"Let me give you some advice worth taking into
discreet consideration, even if you never take any at all
from us. That girl you keep locked in a silent gaze is one
you need to not. She belongs to Ryder, and hell Easton, if

he ever were to catch sight of you looking at her in that way…things won't be so good for you."

I gave an absurd laugh. *"Belongs to Ryder…what do you mean, exactly? What is she a fucking pet?"*

Adam didn't laugh, his brows furrowed as he shook his head. *"Easton, this isn't a joke. It's not some fucking pony ride that when you cry, they let you get off. This is a way of life. The sooner you take it seriously the better off you'll be. Listen… here's a little insight for you regarding the women who hang around the clubhouse and that of any man wearing our cut. Women have no say what so ever! They are advised to keep their mouth shut at all times. Worst way of putting it is they are like a dog and whoever their ol' man is will be the one who is responsible for them. But, only a full patched member can claim a female as we like to call an "ol' lady". Until then, they just hang around like other folks who long to become either a patched member, or for the females, property of a member. Now, a lot of stupid yuppies come crawling when they see us at social gatherings and whatnot. For some reason the damn broads like to be treated as property. I couldn't tell you why when the shit they are forced to do is unlawful and shamefully inhumane."* He paused. *"Just down right awful."*

I scratched at my five o'clock shadow with my other hand rested on my hip. *"Wait…you're saying these females or "hang arounds" like to be disrespected and if not, they are still forced to do things they might not agree with?"*

"Yes. It doesn't matter if they don't want to because if they don't like it, then they probably shouldn't

be here to begin with. And I will tell you this now, no matter what a full patched member tells you or asks you to do…don't you ever be stupid enough to ask why. You had better do it. You have not yet earned the right to claim your own voice. You must show your dedication 100%, no matter how ridiculous it may seem. You are a damn prospect, meaning you do what the fuck you are told and expect to do the dirty work, regardless the legalities. I promise you, the results of disobeying your superiors are far beyond your imagination."

I glanced at the front of my house seeing the porch light still burning. I then gained hope that my mother had not been up all night, worried sick about my whereabouts.

"I guess I can't come up with a good enough reason as to why any woman would want to be "property" of anyone, or anything for that matter."

"Some of them don't have a damn choice and for some, it's all they know. You share that similarity. Shall you soon realize what your life has become, Easton. You have a lot to learn and I hope you take note on every little thing, because that'll be your gateway to freedom. Don't be worried about them ladies, worry about your damn self and what you need to do. That's the best advice I can simply give you."

I snuck into the house making my way straight into my bathroom. Gazing at a newborn outlaw in the mirror wasn't an image my vision wanted to claim. The virtues, the beliefs, and the core values that were instilled in me were no longer present.

My wounded fingertips glided down the leather that clutched my chest like new skin. Everything Ryder had said, even the advice granted by Adam ran vicious circles in my head. Nothing was worse than knowing that what you wanted was far out of your reach. It wasn't so much as freedom I sought…it was *her.*

four

The sudden coolness of my mother's hand rubbing my back caused my eyes to flutter open. Sitting on my bed, she had a worrisome expression marked upon her face.

"Good morning, ma. What's the matter?" I sat up with a yawn.

"Easton, you know how I never dare question your motives. I just have to know that whatever it is that you've been doing lately is safe." Her eyes veered off to the chair blanketed with my cut.

I immediately released a sigh. I hated having to explain things, but this was something I couldn't exactly be in complete honesty about. I conjured up a rough excuse to ease her worried mind. *"Ma, it's nothing. It's just a motorcycle vest."*

"I know what the hell it is, Easton. Don't you dare mock me! I know who those men are and they are no good. What's got you suddenly interested in riding those things anyway? They are extremely dangerous!" A huff flowed from her mouth. *"Was the Corps not enough for you?"*

"Can we discuss my choice of leisure activities later? If I remember correctly, you have a doctor's appointment." I dove from the spotlight; internally begging for her to drop it.

My mother left it at that only for the moment. Though my life was now indemnified to the Keltic Disciples, I wanted to reframe from further unnecessary commination if possible. Watching her car pull out of the drive, I poured myself a cup of coffee before getting ready for the day. I knew it was only minutes before Adam and the rest came tearing through the gravel. Only today, Ryder had showed up along with them.

"All right, pretty boy. We are going to have a little training session for you today. One of our bylaws is that each member must have their own bike. That being only American made machines. Lucky for you, you're not yet fully patched. Therefore, it isn't a requirement. But, in order to be considered a true biker, you must learn to ride one. Have you any experience?"

I didn't want to admit it—God, did I not want to just stand there and shame myself. *"Sadly, no…I have never been on one a day in my life."*

"Ha, what'd I tell you, boss? Nequam." Benjamin crossed his arms over his chest with a snicker.

The lord knew good and well how badly I longed to knock his ass the fuck out.

"We'll see about that. Adam, since you seemed to have volunteered yourself to taxi his ass around, he's your project for the day."

Adam's jaw fell open in astonishment. *"Ryder...you can't be serious? If he drops my bike..."*

"If and when he does drop your bike, you will assist him in picking it back up and teach him until he learns properly. Am I clear?"

"Intelligi..." Adam gritted his teeth.

The duration of my training began in the lot before our clubhouse. I was nervous beyond the point of throwing up the nonexistent contents in my stomach. Other members crowded around to watch my failed attempt to even sit Adam's 800 pound Harley upright without a wobble.

"First things first, take off your fucking cut." Benjamin demanded.

I looked back at the others; confused. They all awaited my move to obey, so I did as instructed. Adam gave a pleased nod, watching me hold it out for Benjamin to grab.

"I don't care to see you drop a member's bike while representing us. You're far from eligible to proudly wear this until you prove to me that you can properly control and handle a task such as this."

I looked down at the bike I straddled, kicking up the kickstand. Searching over the handlebars for an ignition switch, I soon became frustrated.

"You might want to start off by turning it on!" A member yelled sarcastically.

"Easton, pull in your left lever while using your right thumb to press the red ignition switch." Adam instructed.

I did as told, feeling the beast rumble to life between my legs. It shook my entire body as my throat became dry as a bone.

"Now, you're sitting in idle or "neutral". Your left foot when not rested on the foot peg as you would while in motion, there is a lever above it known as the gear shifter. While you continue to keep your left lever in your left hand, you are now holding your clutch. It controls the smooth transition when you enter each gear. Down is first gear, up one notch will place you back into neutral where you will not move if stationary, but can coast while in motion. From there, up one notch would place you into second gear and so on and so forth until you cannot shift upward any further."

Adam had me practice clicking into first gear several times before letting me move forward. Once I was comfortable enough to begin riding slowly, Adam instructed me to ease off the clutch as the bike pulled into first gear and began moving. It jerked forward, startling me as my hands took a vice grip onto the handle grips. My excitement forced my right hand to torque back on the throttle and sent my ass flying forward.

"Easton, slow the fuck down!" Adam called after me.

I looked down at my lap trying to figure out where the damn brakes were. When I found them, it was only the bad news of a train wreck from there. I pulled both levers back as the bike jerked to the left, sending us both straight to the asphalt. I felt the burn of my elbow scrape into the gravel; the bike being stuck on my left leg had Adam rushing over to help me up.

"Jesus irrumabo, Easton! What the fuck were you trying to do?"

I stood to my feet dusting myself off, feeling warm liquid run down the back of my left arm. *"I'm trying to fucking learn how to ride this thing, Adam."*

"Watch your fucking tone and get over here and help me lift er' up!"

Straining until sweat formed on my temples and an ache settled in my lower back did we finally stand the bike back up. Everyone back at the clubhouse just laughed as if I were a pathetic tiger held in captivity, trying to jump through a hoop. The bike had light scratches in the paint, on the gas tank and some scratched into the metal of the bar end. I knew how Adam felt about his bike and now I not only damaged what wasn't mine, but I just made a complete fool of myself in front of everyone—including Adam.

I dug my nails deep into my scalp watching the scorn on Adam's face turn into regretful impatience. *"Get your ass back on and try again."*

I looked stupefied, but I knew I could never question him or anyone else. So I straddled the beast once more, awaiting further instruction. Adam gripped my right shoulder with more pressure than what was comfortable. *"Don't give up, everyone at some point in time has laid their bike down. It isn't if you go down, it's when you go down. You just have to build up your confidence. It's only your first day so I don't expect you to be fucking Evel Knievel. Just take a deep breath and refocus. Your right hand lever is your front brakes your right foot lever is your back brakes. All of your stopping momentum is in the front brakes. It's rare that you are ever forced to use the back brakes, but if you must…be gentle and tap on them. It makes for a smooth and complete stop, so let's try this shit again. And don't worry about them."* He nodded towards the other asinine club members. *"They are laughing at us both, so fuck em'."*

My attention froze on my want that was posted up against the entryway. Her arms crossed over her chest as she watched with a blank stare masqueraded behind sunglasses. I focused my energy and lack of confidence on her, hoping it'd help in the slightest. Restarting the bike, I gently released the clutch as the bike glided into first gear. Using the smallest amount of throttle, I was soon riding in a straight line. It didn't occur to me that sometime soon I'd have to eventually turn around.

In anger and defeat, I stood to my feet with an aggressive groan. My entire left side was busted up so badly with bruises and road rash that I wanted to just give up.

Adam shook his head lending a hand to help stand the bike back up. I was beyond apologetic for the continuous damage that was inflicted on the left hand side.

"It's all right. You just stalled out. That happens when you release the clutch too quickly and are not in the proper gear when attempting to brake. It happens to all of us."

"Woo buddy, if that were my set of wheels I'd be smashing more than that kid's teeth." Benjamin commented.

Ryder came walking out with his perilous ownership clutching to his left arm—not impressed with my failure. *"How's he doing, Adam? By the looks, he is having one hell of a time."*

"He definitely needs a lot of practice. But, he understands the basic fundamentals. He just needs to find confidence and execute the skills instructed."

The arch of her eyebrow raised above the rim of her sunglasses pierced a doubtful hole through my ego. I was now determined more than ever to prove them wrong. I knew I could do this just as easily as I knew I could master the agonizing training of RECON for hours on end. This was no different, it was just another challenge I was faced with until perfected. I chose to spend the hours given to ride around that godforsaken parking lot until my wrists ached and my body grew weak and tired of constant failure.

As the sun met the horizon, I finally completed a full transition through each gear; coming to a complete stop without laying the bike down. The only one who stood proud of my accomplishment was myself. Adam never gave up or lost faith in me, he was more upset over the fact of having to reconstruct his bike.

I am nonesuch and I had to accept that. No matter how many metals I wore, no matter the achievements I was once proud of, none of them mattered now; none of them amounted to a damn thing. I feared no one and nothing...but to catch a glimpse of her eyes, not knowing how it would feel had devoured every ounce of wonder I had left. I had to be near her...even if it caused me to get my ass whooped in front of the entire club, I'd bear it with a smile if it meant having her touch lay upon my flesh. Never in my life had I ever wanted to know someone so badly that I was willing to risk all without a second guess.

"It's getting late. I will take you home."

"Listen, about your bike..." I scratched at my nape.

"Don't worry about it. We all learn through trial and error, do we not?"

I lied awake in my bed as my mind crowded with thoughts I was warned to dissolve. It was impossible; I know what it's like to miss someone...to even want someone, but not like this and not to this extremity. Her mystery tore through me like the blades beneath a harvester. I am a man with high strung confidence to admit what I want and surly have the balls to get it. If she was to go the rest of her life not

ever noticing me, then I have failed no one but my
damn self.

****

I stood behind the bar cleaning the same glass
over and over, staring through it to watch those defined
legs nestled in heels as they clacked across the
hardwood. Resting a hand atop Ryder's shoulder, they
soon met eyes before she rested in his lap. I began
solving algebra problems in my head to keep my hard-
on at a bare minimum. The way she giggled while
running her hand up and down Ryder's chest, casually
sipping on the glass of Merlot I recently poured had my
nerves set on edge. Her lips met the scruff of his face
while she whispered sweet nothings to arouse him as his
grip intensified against her bare thigh. I was lost in
their interaction, longing for it to be me that she was
carelessly feeling up on. To read in on every word that
escaped the sweetness of her lips as the flesh of my chest
hardened with tremendous flexion. Saliva built up in
my cheeks until a member walked up demanding a
beer.

"Heus, te nequam irrumabo." He slurred. *"Get
me another lager."*

I popped open his desired bottle but before
releasing it, my eyes locked on his. *"If you don't mind
explaining, what the fuck does "nequam" mean?"*

He just gave a sardonic laugh, yanking the
bottle from my grip. *"I will tell you this… if you look at
me like that again, I'll break your goddamn neck."*

I puffed out a rugged breath, dropping my rag on the bar top before making my way to the cooler. Secured behind the metal door, I slammed my back against the wall with belligerence. I needed a moment to regain my self-control before carrying two large cases full of beer. Why uphold a real occupation when you can slave beneath the boot of a bunch of outlawed bikers for the rest of your fucking life?

I yanked up two cases of Bud and made my way back down the dim hallway. Along the way, the door to Ryder's office was slightly cracked. I never had the opportunity to gander inside, but maybe it was for the best considering what I saw disturbed the final nerve of restraint left within me.

There she was….on her knees with a mouth full. I saw Ryder's hand with the same iron rings he always wore, gliding through light strands of hair, easing into a grip to shove himself in further.

I curled up a nostril as my eyes narrowed. *"What can I get you, gentlemen?"* My jaw clenched.

I recognized one as 'Quaestor' as his nametape read 'Treasurer' beneath. *"A shot of Jack and a change in your fucking attitude, nequam."*

I tossed up a shot glass, filling it to the rim; accidentally spilling some over. As I slid it in his direction, his expression was all but accepting. *"Clean up the fucking mess. Someone needs to teach you how to pour a man a fucking shot!"*

Wanting to block out every word he was saying was just wishful thinking. Tossing the shot back, he slammed the glass down asking for me to pour several more for the rest of the members who stood by. I took a deep breath lining up the tiny glasses while running the bottle across each one until all were filled to the rim. It was impossible to not have some spillage, but these guys didn't give a fuck if it was or wasn't; they wanted to harass me because they could.

"I do believe the man asked you to clean it up!"

My eyes shot forward only to land upon the ill-tempered Benjamin, himself. His hand quickly snatched the back of my neck, slamming my face down into the amber puddle. Reaching forward with my rag to sop up the mess, Benjamin yanked it from my grasp, pressing his fingers deeper into my neck until I released a squeal.

"Stick out your fucking tongue." He demanded through gritted teeth.

It was unbearable to remain in this position, but even if I had rolled my tongue from my mouth, it wouldn't have made much of a difference. Refusing an order was a mistake around here and I knew it, but I still didn't budge for I was stubborn... or maybe just plain stupid.

"I guess he didn't fucking hear me." Benjamin whipped out a pocket knife, resting the blade rather firmly against my jawline. *"If you do not stick out your tongue, I will remove it from your fucking mouth, myself!"*

With an agitated groan, I released my tongue from my mouth as he shoved my face harder into the liquid. Maiming me in front of the entire club as the punished puppy whose nose was being shoved in piss, I wanted to shove his knife straight through his fucking throat.

"Quod Satis!" Ryder yelled.

A hand took the collar of my shirt to stand me upright.

"You got lucky this time." Benjamin snarled before tossing his drink back. Turning the shot glass completely upside down, he ensured that the final drop of whiskey landed on the bar top before clanking it down.

The bitter liquid ran down my lips as I licked them shamefully. In the distance, I saw Adam rested against the pool table in distress. I now realized that I was Adam's prospect, I was his responsibility and yet, I was doing a damn good job of letting him down. Something had to give and it sure as hell needed to happen now.

Because of the mayhem or rather 'disturbance' I had caused earlier on, I had to stay late once again to close down the bar. I knelt down wiping the coolers clean until I could see my murky reflection across the stainless steel.

The sound of the jukebox startled me as I slowly poked my head just above the edge of the bar top to gain a visual. It was who I only unexpectedly hoped for. The way she carried her carefree sway let me know she thought she was alone.

As she danced around in circles while singing into her half emptied beer bottle, a giggle rumbled deep within my throat. I knew I couldn't remain crouched behind the bar all evening, so I slowly stood to my feet while busying myself drying freshly cleansed glasses. A smile pulled up the right side of my face being the only witness of her self-choreographed habitual presentation. Once she noticed my existence, she nearly jumped from her skin instantly placing a hand to her heaving chest.

"Shh… no one else is in here besides us." I said calmly.

She was quick to regain her emotions, taking a long pull from her bottle. *"How long have you been standing there gazing upon my movement like you always do?"*

Her question backed me into a corner and I could hardly swallow. *"How do you figure I always watch you?"*

"Oh please," She laughed taking several confident steps towards me. *"Because, Mr. Ruckett. I see all. I never say much to anyone, but I see more than what others think. Like your constant stare that lingers through every little thing I do."*

I felt my breathing slow as I watched her lips while she spoke. *"With all due respect, I cannot help but to watch you."*

"Well, you need to regain control." Her expression hardened.

"Why?"

"Because, I know my place and I respect the position of those around me. Which you need to do the same before getting your ass beat. I am even taking a

grave risk exchanging words with the one they've branded with "nequam"." A devilish grin danced across her lips.

"What does that even mean?" I became tense.

"It's just another nickname they've come up with to gain dominance over you... like the rest of us."

I slightly wetted my lips trying to ease my nerves. *"What do they call you?"*

Her eyes reacquainted mine as she chugged the remaining liquid inside her bottle. Sliding it in my direction, she paused just as I took ahold of its neck. *"Susurri..."* The syllables fell nimble from her mouth.

I shook my head not quite understanding. *"Look, if you haven't noticed, I don't speak Latin. Therefore, I do not comprehend it, either."*

Leaning in closer towards my face, she curled her index finger to draw me in. *"It means 'whisper'. I am not to speak to anyone except Ryder. He is as they say, my ol' man. You don't want to know the beginning of what he and the others will do to you if we are ever caught communicating. But, for the record...yes, I do see you look at me even though you really shouldn't."*

"I find it merely impossible." I admitted weakly.

"Find a possibility before you make matters worse... for the both of us." She warned before exiting the clubhouse.

I finished lining up the glasses in a straight row before meeting Adam outside. He and a few other members of our board or 'chain of command' were busy conversing about business over a social smoke. Susurri glanced back in my direction after straddling the back of Ryder's bike. I wasn't jealous of the man because I'd never dare to consider her property, but damn if she belonged to me then I'd understand why he didn't want anyone speaking with her or passing a subtle glance. She isn't like the rest of the 'yuppies' as they call them who hang around full patch holders, begging for some sense of entitlement when they really should rethink on what it means to be a fucking lady.

Everything about Susurri would have any man in here crawling on his hands and knees just to have a taste. Somehow, I lucked out with slight conversation...but that wasn't enough. Our little talk was merely the spark of drawing out deeper wants, the same ones I was forced to withhold for my own good and apparently that of hers, too. I was going to find a way to have her...I just didn't know how exactly.

𝕱𝖎𝖛𝖊

𝕱or the past three nights I have had the privilege of taking private riding lessons with Adam during afterhours. He wanted to ensure that I'd be halfway ready for the long haul up to Lexington for a rally meet. According to Adam, the Disciples must make appearances at social gatherings prominently. He said 'how is anyone to fear us if we never show ourselves-- especially unexpectedly?' I guess I could make sense of what he was implying. There were supposed to be over

700 other bikers at this rally Kentucky sponsored annually. I was happy not having to ride bitch for my first meet, but I still have yet to go out and purchase a bike for myself. Instead, Adam allowed me to borrow his Harley Street 750. It was light enough for me to handle on a two and a half hour ride. I was pretty excited to coast a few miles instead of playing around in a damn parking lot.

Standing before the mirror in my bathroom, I took ahold of my razor gazing at my face skeptically. A little stubble never hurt nobody, though I wasn't used to having the edgy look only ever being able to keep it for no more than 48 hours over a weekend.

I cleaned up my jawline and left a faint circle beard. The lighting illuminated glacier irises while I gave a snug jerk to my cut. As my eyes danced over the nametape that marked me as 'prospect', I couldn't help but optimize the meaning behind 'nequam'; or at least what I thought it meant. I had to prove a lot of dedication to these guys; I just didn't know where to even begin.

I quietened my steps into the kitchen as much as a pair of ropers would allow. While awaiting Adam and the others, I turned on the teapot for my mother when Draper came pulling up. With his famous backwoods grin of a bear eating honey, he came jolting up to the porch door rather chipper this morning.

"Hey, what are ya up to today?" His overbearing smile presented malicious conception.

"I have a meeting to attend in Kentucky." I replied plainly.

"Oh? Did you land a job or something?"

"…Not exactly." I nervously took a sip of tea, scolding my mouth in the process.

"You get yourself a honey up there?" He joked.

I rolled my eyes with a smirk. *"If only. Anyway, you gonna tell me what you're all jubilant about so damn early?"*

"I have two tickets to see Florida Georgia Line and since you enjoy their stuff I figured you'd like to tag along."

"Sounds like a great time, but I'm gonna have to take a rain check."

His smile instantly dropped into a frown. *"Oh…I just haven't seen you much since you've come home. I just want to spend time with my best friend. Hell, you are even beginning to dress like them."*

"Well damn, Draper. When you say it like that…"

"Don't worry about it. We can get up another time when you're free." He forced a smile.

My expression darkened as I stared through him, watching several bikes pull up before my house. His attention followed as his reaction bled hysterical confusion.

"So, that thing I have to attend is about to take place. I will give you a call when I get back in town."

"Are you seeking to be some hardcore biker, now? Easton, those kinds of people…"

"Those kinds of people? Listen to yourself. They are just the same as you and I. Don't be so quick to judge."

Draper followed me out the front door still ranting about my forced lifestyle. *"The Keltic Disciples? Lord, you must be joking!"*

"What?" I turned around with attitude.

"I wouldn't be as concerned if you were riding a motorized scooter with a bunch of California babes, but you're not! The Disciples are a biker gang, Easton. I understand that the Corps was pretty intense and full of outrageous excitement, but if you're seeking thrill beyond legal expense then smoke some marijuana."

I shrugged off his worrisome banter as Adam slid off his bike. *"Is this cat bothering you, Easton?"*

"No, no! He's good people. This is Draper. He's an old friend of mine."

Draper stood timidly fearful to even speak further once Adam closed in the distance between them. *"Just be safe, Easton, and call me as promised."* He pulled his hat down further to shield his identity.

I watched him hurry back to his car, peeling off.
I wasted no time by hopping on the back of Adam's
bike. My blood was rushing with excitement to straddle
a bike all on my own. All of our club members were
gathered before the clubhouse, mingling about while
others continued to show up. Everyone's bikes were
lines up accordingly by rank. I had to ride further back
due to my pitiful position, but I was determined to rise
up—unexpectedly. A man can dream, right?

A leather jacket, tight black leggings and wedges
to match a ruling persona, Susurri strutted across the
lot with another female I have yet to become acquainted
with. She was not one to catch my interest, but her smile
forced me to return the gesture. Pointing in my
direction for I stood close to high rankings, it caused a
lot of attention from other members. Susurri followed
her finger but was quick to contain a blank expression
behind sunshades; just as she always had when looking
my way. It set my hormones on a frenzied rage even
though she wanted little to nothing to do with me. But, I
loved it. Feening relentlessly for her to waltz past me
just to breathe her in, to feel her braze lightly against
my skin had my mouth salivating. My groin pulsed
beneath my jeans like a restless steed, but I stood
unmoved.

Ryder gained everyone's attention giving the
itinerary a rundown before rolling out. Releasing us to
start our bikes, Adam walked me over to my new
transportation. For a moment, I was stuck in place
watching Ryder loop his arms around Susurri's hips,

pulling her into him as he planted a kiss on her neck. Lost in a daydream, a sudden force crashed into me bringing me back to reality. It was Benjamin rudely shoving his way past me as if *I* was in his way.

"Move, nequam pungunt!" He sneered while spitting down at my feet.

"Look, I know you are still in your learning stage. But, learning on a bike has a lot of grey areas. When riding in a pack, you have no grey areas. You must conduct proper road rules and signs. Pay attention to all signals given ahead to reduce the risk of an accident. I've seen one guy make a mistake and took out at least twenty other bikers, so it is important. You'll get the hang of it the more you ride. Fortunatos." He smiled.

"What?"

"In other words, good luck. And just a suggestion, you may want to brush up on your Latin terminology. It will take you twice as long just to learn by ear around here. Plus, it gives great advantage to know our heritage and language. Soon, you'll be able to properly enunciate and have a silver tongue with the ladies, just remember your position." Adam dropped the keys into my palm, leaving me to figure out the rest on my own as he moved towards the front of the pack to take his position.

I slid the key into the ignition letting the bike rattle between my legs. It was a nice leisure to have, but lonesome if no one was rested on the back; comforting you with the security of their arms. Giving us the signal,

Ryder and Benjamin led the lines as we began our journey.

Cruising down the interstate with eighty other people who carried the same belief and purpose felt like the closest thing to a fleet of marching soldiers ready for battle, though this was more like a dysfunctional family. I took my time and paid as close attention as possible with the wind suffocating me. The time it took to arrive to our destination wasn't as long as I had anticipated. On a large grassy plane sat hundreds of motorcycles and tents with bodies scattered about. We had our own designated parking area— where ever the fuck we felt like.

I slid off the bike, shoving the keys deep into my pocket trying to mask my nervousness of being in an unfamiliar setting. Though it was easy to adjust having a history of setting foot onto others territory, being the uninvited, the terrorist and the unwanted. Strangers representing different clubs were spread about the premises, drinking and socializing. Ryder claimed to hardly ever mingle with the 99%ers, but we did what we had to just to maintain our reputation.

A venue with hundreds of variations of patches caught my attention. I absentmindedly made my way towards it, glancing over different styles and creatures that many bikers wore on their cut. I saw everything from half naked women, words of slander and plenty of skulls with crossbones. It wasn't really my style, or in any likes of what I would want to display. Instead, my eyes stopped on a group of cluttered military branch patches. I picked one up that represented my prior service, staring through it as if it was transparent.

"Devil dog, are you?"

The owner of the venue broke my train of thought. *"Excuse me?"*

"A Devil dog… you're holding a Semper Fi patch, I just assumed you're a Marine."

"Was." I corrected. To skip the small talk of how many tours I had served, I instead asked how much for the patch of superiority.

"$5, but for you, I'll do it for $3 considering your appreciated service." He stared at me for a moment. *"Also, congrats on prospecting. It isn't an easy thing to accomplish."* His side smirk left me to do the same.

I pressed my lips together feeling a presence lurk dangerously close. My eyes followed the hand that reached out taking ahold of a studded bracelet. Susurri had an innocent smirk, but never turned directly towards me.

"Latin…I'm impressed."

"It's probably the only Latin I know." I chuckled.

Suddenly, an unfamiliar hand ran up my back and through my hair. *"Quam bella?"* A woman's voice intimately giggled.

I couldn't read Susurri's expression behind her sunglasses, but she seemed unthreatened. The same woman I caught her walking with at the clubhouse appeared behind me. As we began conversing, I watched Susurri hand the venue owner a $20 bill.

"Nere eum esse hominem , amabo?"

I didn't know what she said, but damnit did I find it undeniably sexy when she'd speak in Latin—or when she spoke, period. The vendor requested my vest and began sewing on my patch. I turned to thank her; she just patted me on the back whispering 'non omittere' before walking off.

"Careful now, she is a marked woman. I, on the other hand am not."

"And you are?" I arched a peculiar brow.

"Moira..." She smiled brightly. *"It means "the great"."* She directed into my ear.

"I'm prospect, Easton Ruckett."

"Excellent introduction, but I already know who you are, baby."

"You do?" I reached out to grab my cut.

My new patch, the only one that held meaning to me was placed on my left hand side; aligned with my second button. I smoothed my hand over it with pride while Moira continued talking.

"It's hard not to notice the caged bull that is stubborn beyond his right."

I became sternly defensive under my breath. *"You know nothing about me…"*

"Say's the one they call "nequam"." She laughed tauntingly.

I wanted to snap, I even found myself envisioning my hand clasped tightly around her fucking neck just to shut her up. Removing myself from a possible conflict, I made my way over to a nearby beer trailer. Of course the broad followed me, so to be a gentleman I handed her a bottle as well. Just as I went to place mine to my lips, a hand smacked it out of my grasp as it fell to the grass in a foamy mess.

"What the fuck?"

"Watch your fucking mouth! You think you can just buy any female a goddamn drink?" Benjamin snapped.

The look of satisfaction filled Moira's eyes as a devilish smile clung to her mouth the way her hands clung to his right bicep. A set up? How classy. I respectfully knelt down before him to pick up the bottle. The moment he stepped on my hand was the very moment I had to specifically choose on whether I wanted to live to see another day or not. My eyes reached my reflection in his glasses as he took a hand to my collar, bringing me to his face.

"Semper Fi, huh? What are you always faithful to, nequam? Besides pissing me off, I doubt you honor any other fucking values."

That remark alone hit me hard with a punch to the gut. You can say what the fuck you want about me, but to question my faith and honor to my country and history of service was yet another. But if I give in by punching him in the jaw, who was winning here? He wanted a rise out of me; he wanted to find what pissed me off the most. Granted, he deserved an ass beating from any Marine, now was not the time to display such negligence. His time would come and I'd make sure he begged for my mercy, regretting everything he's ever said to me.

Getting lost in the crowd after replacing my beer, a live band took the stage covering some old ZZ Top hits. I bobbed my head to the beat minding my own business when I captured Susurri and Moira dancing in a group of hippish female riders. To break my strain of infatuation, Adam shoulder bumped me holding out a pair of sunglasses and a wallet attached to a chain.

"What is this for?" My brows drew together.

"Well for one, if you're going to keep staring into the "sun" you may need some eye protection. Secondly, it's never safe to keep cash on hand like you do, so I picked this up from a buddy I know."

I glanced down at the wallet inscribed with an eagle, globe, and anchor. A distant smile of humble gratitude pulled my cheeks back for a brief moment. *"Adam...thank you."*

"It's gratias, and you're welcome." He smirked. *"Now, put those damn shades on before someone blackens those eyes for the intent staring problem you've acquired."*

I slid on my visual safety specs, placing my money safely into the fold of my new leather wallet. The chain hung comfortably against my right thigh, bringing more attention to the ripped Levi's I chose to wear. Interrupting our conversation, a few members from another 1%er club had the audacity to curl up a lip to attempt a prohibited exchanging of words. Two men and a woman stood before Adam and I as if we owed them something beyond a 'can I fucking help you?'.

"So, I bet these guys have you sucking a lot of dick just to wear that pretty little cut of yours." One laughed.

I looked to Adam for help, knowing it was forbidden and written in our bylaws to never associate with other 1%ers who were not either members from other chapters of the Keltic Disciples, or members of our sub-group who answered to us. He raised his hand, running his finger along the new addition on my leather. I sensed danger, maybe even a deep threat but I didn't have to say a damn thing because Adam's fist cracked him across the jaw so hard a tooth was knocked loose.

"He is my property! He does not answer to you or anyone else who is not a Disciple, you lupatriae filius! You know better than to touch a prospect that is not of your own!"

Realizing a commotion had broken out; Ryder and Benjamin were quick to intervene. If Adam's punch to the face wasn't enough of a warning, Benjamin immediately tagged himself in and beat the living shit out of this guy. Wrestling him to the ground, Benjamin had the advantage and wailed on him until Ryder tried pulling him off. Benjamin is not a very tall man, though he is stout and full of muscle. I wanted to help but Adam wouldn't allow me to move.

"Let this be a lesson, one in which should warn any mother fucker who dares to commence some bullshit like that, again. Mind your fucking business and get the hell away from my brothers." Ryder warned.

Susurri and Moira came busting through to check on us…well, to check on Benjamin and Ryder— of course. Looking my way longer than she ever has, I felt her concern radiate through the polarization of her lenses. It literally sent a shockwave through my heart, driving me further into the suffocation of desperation. Having the slightest incentive of grasping the tiny element in which held solicitude had my heart burning embers strong enough to deteriorate graphene. Did she know she already had me? Was she aware of the power she held over me though we have never touched or admitted such things?

"Who the fuck were those guys?"

"Nobody you need to worry about." Ryder answered before rounding everyone up.

"They are members of the Sick Sixth Sins that run Kentucky. We may have been in their territory, but they knew better than to start something with us. Besides,

it was a public event, so their colors and our colors only
hold verbal value and the integrity of those who wear
them." Adam informed.

      I gave one last look over my shoulder watching
them pull out, revving obnoxiously past us along the
way. Ryder gave them the finger with a smile and kept
on going. These guys didn't seem so bad; then again it
wasn't me who had pissed them off this time.

Six

Blasting grunge music without any consideration of my mother, I knelt down beside my bed pulling out a lockbox that contained my millennium G2 .9mm; along with my concealed license buried beneath. It hasn't been fired in several months, but it was clean and ready for war if need be. Sliding it into its holster, I placed the box back underneath my bed before exiting my room. My mother was seated at the kitchen table reading the paper as usual; only she did not look in my direction as I entered the room. I could sense that something wasn't right, but I feared to ask what it was.

Pondering the beginning of a much needed conversation, I poured myself a glass of water before plopping down across from her. As her eyes rose slowly from the paper, up my cut and into my eyes, I could barely swallow. I knew she saw my patch and she didn't comment; she only smiled.

"I apologize for the disturbance of unnecessary loud music, earlier."

"Easton, it's fine."

"No it isn't..." I sighed. *"Ma, what is going on?"*

"The doctor wants me to get a cat scan." She responded without hesitation.

My eyes enlarged, fearing the worst. *"W—what for, exactly?"*

"Don't take it too heavily. He just wants to ensure that everything is healthy as it should be."

I silently nodded while tanking down my glass of water. All I could think about was what if they did find something? What if it wasn't just potential loss of memory, that maybe it was a tumor of some sort— cancer even. I shook the horrific possibility away as best I could until I knew further.

"Do you want me to take you to your appointment? 'Cause I can…"

"You have other things you need to focus on. Don't worry about me."

"That's like telling me to not breathe, ma. I will take you because I want to. It isn't a damn chore to take care of my mother!"

"Still that restless tone, Easton. Okay, you can take me. It's tomorrow morning at 9."

"Yes ma'am. I got to get going, my ride is here."

As I stood to leave, my mother halted my movement. *"Easton…"*

"Ma'am?" I answered over my shoulder.

My mother paused for a long moment, but changed her mind. I had a feeling I knew what she wanted to say, maybe she shared the same fear of knowing what I was up to recently, just as I was fearful of what was going on with her. Distancing myself probably wasn't the best solution, then again I didn't have the choice of free will an average man should. I wasn't average. I was a product not of my own design, but that of the devil himself who was peculiarly taking his time to mold me in the way he wanted me to be. I was dense, but not ignorant. I just shielded myself in the way I was taught through provision and organized structure.

Today was unlike any day I have endured at the clubhouse so far. All of the members of our board were lined up out front. The last person I wanted to see was the very first to approach me with his insolent bullshit. I was bold enough to place my hands upon my hips like I deserved to stand on the ground trapped beneath my boots—I was dead wrong.

"Nice to see that you've become Adam's little "canis puer"…I don't give a shit. Yet, you dare stand before me as if you have any sense of entitlement." Benjamin's eyes darted down towards my belt line. *"Ha, what's this?"* He reached his hand out to take ahold of my pistol I failed to properly conceal.

Instinctively as any cop or Marine would, I grabbed his hand out of pure reaction. His bottom jaw dropped open as if he was taken aback by my courageous strike. Cocking his head over his shoulder he yelled 'habet a gun' and suddenly a handful of members came rushing outside to see what the fuss was about.

Reacquainting my eyes, his stare narrowed as his grip tightened around my pistol. I did not budge as I recited my rifle creed in my head for the millionth time on record. Looking through him, I watched Ryder and Susurri run to the edge of the steps of the veranda.

Crossing his arms over his chest, Ryder paused his movement.

"You know what to do, Benjamin. Tractandi."

My moment of weakness damn near cost me my life. In a split second, Benjamin had yanked my pistol from its holster, cocked the slider leaving the familiar sound of a bullet entering the chamber to ring loudly in my ears. The gun was soon pressed into my chest as a sadistic grin painted across his smug ass face. I took a moment to calm my nerves as my heart pounded against my ribs. I have been here before, but with an AK-47 pressed against my temple. I dared myself to not show defeat, nor fell victim to become a prisoner of war. I looked my enemy in the eyes with the defiance of dilated pupils, silently praying that if I were to die, God would forgive my failure.

"You have your own pistol held to your chest, yet you refuse to fight for your life? Hmm…why does this all look so familiar? Oh yes, I remember…this is exactly how Eden felt the night you used his own weapon to defeat him. How does it feel to be on the opposing end?"

I was damned if I allowed myself to continue standing there letting him belittle my means for survival. So, I did what I do best—I fought back. I slung my left arm over his, grabbing the pistol with both hands while turning my back into him. Using my weight as a force of momentum, I reared back against him slamming us both down onto the ground. He refused to let go of the pistol, squeezing the trigger sending a bullet off into the air. I heard the frequency of a few females who shrilled while covering their ears.

Susurri stood in obvious fright with parted lips. Rolling up onto my feet covered in dust, I watched

Benjamin stand to his with my pistol still pointed in my direction. Closing in the space between us, I felt the warmth of the barrel pressed into my temple. Panting, unable to catch my breath I saw rage burning in Benjamin's retinas.

"I did what I had to…" I raised my hands respectfully.

"Did what you had to? Well, mother fucker…I guess I'm just doing what should have been done the night you nearly took the life of one of our brothers! He may not have meant a goddamn thing to you, but he did to me and fuck you for that!"

"Benjamin! Prohibere!"

"Boss, you said to handle this, so I am."

"Not by death, you will not!"

Not removing his eyes from me, Benjamin dropped the clip from my gun, unloaded the bullet and slammed the pistol into my chest. *"Just remember…te vita mea."*

As he turned to walk away, I dropped my pistol to the ground taking off after him. If I knew one thing, I knew 'vita' meant life and that was something he did not have and never would.

I dug my hands into his shoulders slamming him down to the ground. I lost myself, my self-control, my values and virtues meant nothing at that point. This was between me and him and it had been a long time coming. I needed to show the bastard that I would decide on how far anyone could go with me.

Left and right, I pounded my fists into him out of anger. Blood covered his face as he tried throwing me off of him. Before it was too late, Adam swooped in pulling me from my true enemy. I scrambled to break free as the Disciples who stood by clamored for more. It was a risk that I took, but one well worth it.

Ryder ran down picking Benjamin up from the ground before dealing with me.

"You think because you have a gun, it makes you more of a man? Or the fact you possess proper self-defense skills that you are an outstanding Marine? Take a look around, you are no longer in the service. You answer to me! As much as you hate it, your life is ours! You chose your fate the night you injured Eden. If you ever pull a stunt like that again, I can promise your suffering will be far beyond your fucking dreams!" Just like that, Ryder raised his hand full of iron rings and backhanded me so hard blood shot from my nose and onto the ground. *"Remember your place, Easton. You have no rights, you have earned nothing. You are no one but who I fucking say you are. I am your superior, Benjamin is second in line. You do as your told and just maybe your life won't be so difficult. I can give a flying fuck about what you've been through. I don't care what you've seen, who you've lost or the things you had to do to "survive". This club is your priority, your family, your fucking life and you will learn how to control yourself. How dare you disrespect your chain of command like this! What would*

*your commander or your sergeant do if you pulled a stunt
like that?"*

*"It would be punishable, because it could cost
more than just my own life."*

*"You're damn right it would. I now introduce
you to Chad, our Sergeant at Arms. He is the muscle of
this club if and whenever we need him. I will teach you to
step out of line again. Chad, et huc venerunt."* He
commanded.

He and two other members came walking up
with a rope braided in the colors of our club. I have
seen many riders have these hanging on their right
handlebar, though I assumed it was for decoration.
The heavyweight blondie motioned for his two
accomplices to hold me down on my knees in front of
everyone. With crass, Chad stripped me from my cut,
throwing it to the dirt before ripping my shirt off. Both
members were designated to hold each of my arms
while Chad commenced public chastisement, flogging
me for punishment. Rolling the whip out, the slap of its
end cracked through my soul, completely shattering
every ounce of pride I thought I had.

*"Et amplexatur sustinere and you shall survive
the pain."* Chad suggested.

The crack of the whip split into my skin as
blood soon dripped from continuous strikes. My eyes
cried mercy, but my mind gained the willpower to
withstand such brutality by looking Susurri dead on
due to my transgression. From our distance, I could see
the blush upon her cheeks, though for the first time her

eyes were not hidden. I looked directly into them as she never dared looking away from mine. Each time the whip hit me I forced myself to grin and bear it, envisioning myself only getting closer and closer to her. I may have embarrassed myself, made a fool out of whatever dignity I had left, but even at that distance, if it meant getting to look Susurri in the eyes then damn my soul and the life I claimed. Because, I'd do anything to be stuck…to be lost in her gaze no matter how obscene the reality of it really was.

Clouds rolled in and thunder rumbled across the atmosphere as light droplets began falling. It stung my back at first, but I embraced the coolness against my wounded flesh that was on fire. If this wasn't a lesson well learned, then I didn't know what the fuck would be. I began to question if I really wanted to continue a lustrous want for a woman who would never be mine, but love might have been the only token that kept me clinging on tight. I had to change my way of thinking, these guys were overpowering in numbers and experience. Though, I knew nothing about what it truly meant to be a biker…I did know about brotherhood. They took it more seriously than a fucking fraternity, this was everything to them and I did a great job disrespecting one of the highest ranking people here.

Had fallen into a deep slumber, a foot kicking me in the gut awoken me rather quickly. I opened my eyes to see Adam standing over me presenting my cut and a helping hand. Struggling to stand, I looked at him with confusion.

"I cannot bear watching this shit go on. It is time you learn about us and where we originally came from. I could not save you from punishment, though I damn well hope you learned your fucking lesson. Next time will not be so easy."

"Oh of course not, what is easier than being whipped in front of your entire club?"

"Always finding a way to be a smartass...let's start there. All punishment is not always granted physically."

"Meaning?"

"Meaning, they will punish you in different ways. Forcing you to do things you can't even imagine. I've seen some horrific shit. I have been put in positions where I was left with the fucking obvious choice. You either do it, or die. If you are not willing to die for these guys, or suffer legal consequence then you don't belong here. In your case you have no choice, therefore you had better shut the fuck up and do as you are told."

For hours, Adam sat explaining the history of the club. Apparently the Keltic Disciples originated in Ireland back in 1939, only starting with several men and their wives at the time. Ardan O'Kane was the original founder; his name alone meant 'high aspiration'. His outlook on life was hazy considering the illegal travel he and his members had to make through Europe during World War II. After migrating safely to Rome, Ardan was branded with 'Deus Libertatis' meaning God of freedom.

Subsequently residing in Rome's capital, their Irish tongue soon transitioned into Latin as a new found language. The Roman Republic refused to permit any law for a gang of bikers that ran wild throughout the city and that of Europe.

Due to conflict with government and local authority who threatened to exile Ardan and his family from Europe, in 1946 all members boarded a ship immigrating to the Northeast part of America where the invention of a concrete foundation for a legal motorcycle club was lawful. Later, the name Keltic Disciples was agreed upon and used as their identifier.

The club patch was not created until the 1950's whereas members originally wore a Celtic cross on the back of their leather vests with the club name written above in old English. The usage of MC on their riding vest was implemented to present the fact of being considered 1%ers, embracing the biker lifestyle. It also informs authority that anyone who wears the MC patch and/or the 1%er diamond on their jacket/vest verified possible organized crime and rejection to any law enforcement.

Ardan believed freedom did not come without cost and victory was not obtained without great sacrifice, so encouraged living to conquer the entirety of one's wants, regardless of retaliation and disagreement through disorderly conduct.

The latter days of the 1960's, into the early 70's the Keltic Disciples become nationwide, known to all bikers across the country. Most people feared them and did not think twice to intervene while members were in the area. Having accumulated both MC and 1%er diamond patches for hardcore representation, a

member named Eden Ahern created the club's colors.
The Celtic cross soon became one imbedded with Celtic
knots with the Celtic Triquetra centered. The
Triquetra in most cases stood for the power of three in a
religious realm. Ardan and Eden believed differently
about the definition and decided that all points of their
Triquetra would only represent 'creation, preservation,
and destruction'.

The usage of a Celtic knot was desirable through
a remembrance of where they came from. The club's
name alone means 'followers of Irish origin'. The knot
expresses 'endlessness' in which has neither beginning
nor end. Intertwining the unsubtlety of turquoise as the
knot's color, Ardan wanted a symbol upholding
tradition and the value of uninterrupted life cycle while
enduring longevity, luck and new endeavors.

The colors of turquoise and gray were chosen
specifically because of their meaning, turquoise is
considered an emotional roller coaster until finding
balance. It is said to recharge inner spirit during times
of mental stress and tiredness. It has the power to
alleviate feelings of loneliness, while assisting in
development of organization and management. The
only color that influences rather than demands. The
trueness of brotherhood is recognized through this
color.

Gray is the shade of indecisiveness as it stands to
be the equalizer. It is unemotionally detached,
impartial, yet solid with stability while releasing relief
from chaos. Placing these colors together was an
ingenious impact to all members who voted upon

substantial agreement.

To finalize the patch for completion, two red ovals were placed behind the cross as a reminder of their bloodline and tradition for it runs deep, never accepting the substitution of a traitor or the ignorance of deprivation, embracing the trials of difficulty for glory prevailed. Respect is not given, it is earned and anyone who disagreed was not cut out to ride with the true Disciples, much less 'hang around'.

After doing a little research of my own, I was in complete bewilderment realizing that the man I stabbed at the bar was in fact one of the oldest members of the club. Being an outsider clarifies nothing beyond an innocent thought along with ignorant assumptions. Brotherhood meant everything to these guys and nothing or no one was going to get in the way of what they believed in.

As for a former Marine, I was trained to believe that honor and glory ran deeper than my bones, yet it is only the shined surface of a fresh burn. Peel back a few layers and just maybe you will find what it means to belong somewhere and to be loved beyond the person you stand to be with the purpose you carry.

Seven

It wasn't the fact of a sleepless night that had me cringing, but the brownish streaks stained into my sheets were another addition to my irritation. The lashes laid thick into my back refused to keep closed, so for every hyper extensive stretch—my skin would rip open, leaving my cuts to ooze and burn. I've bled through three shirts and I knew in time, my mother would catch on asking what the hell had happened to me. I couldn't remain sour over the fact that it was in her nature, I just didn't have an accurate explanation for this.

To my advantage, my mother was sound asleep on the couch with a book rested on her chest. I stood in the doorway silently admiring the look of peace instilled in her dreaming expression. As easy as possible, I removed the book placing it onto the coffee table beside her. As little as I have been around lately, I have missed her more than the Tennessee air, itself. My mother didn't deserve to be lied to; then again she didn't deserve to be placed in harm's way, either.

Stretching the screen door open, the world welcomed me as the sun's rays warmed my face, only to scorch through the leather, searing my back. I took a long look at Adam's motorcycle, the very same one he had been letting me borrow for the past week. Eventually, I had to get myself a set of wheels; I just didn't know a damn thing about them in order to do so.

Throwing my right leg over to straddle the beast, the motor roared to life sending ticklish vibrations through my thighs. Pulling up to the clubhouse, I longed to see only one face. The only one who has kept me sane during this brutal journey thus far. Adam greeted me with a beer and a firm hand shake as I walked through the door. Inhaling secondhand smoke was not something I longed to do for the next twenty minutes, so

I instead began my daily ritual of bar duties while everyone else simmered down for a meeting.

Susurri was rested directly beside Ryder, as always. I couldn't help but to raise a nostril each time I had to endure watching them interact. It was torturous, not to mention heartbreaking to witness the one you want so badly, falling all over another out of your comparison. Burrowing my fist deep inside a mug to cleanse away water spots, my eyes met the deacon with the thirst of rage and new order. Benjamin drew in a deep breath through his nostrils while taking a masculine grip to his genitals. His shades covered the black eye I marked him with and I felt myself smiling inside. I wasn't sure what the fuck he was insinuating, but lesson well learned...you don't shit where you eat.

Running an arrogant tongue across the top row of his teeth, Benjamin made his way over to me. I prepared myself for the worst because no matter how pissed off he got me, I was completely defenseless. I could lay into him with every word in my vocabulary, I could hit him in every pressure point of his stature, yet he will always rise from the ashes to overpower me.

"Well hello there, nequam. Make yourself fucking useful and pour me some amber."

"Anything specific, Benjamin?" I clenched my jaw.

"Jameson." He replied briskly.

I turned to grab the bottle, tossing three ice cubes into a rocks glass watching him lean his elbow onto the bar top. *"So, how are those lashes feeling today?"*

I really wanted to ask him about his black eye and busted lip, but I chose to bite my tongue. *"I'm sure you can use your imagination."* I sneered.

Sliding the glass over in Benjamin's direction, he took a quick grab to my wrist. Never leaving my eyes, a fiendish smile raised the right side of his face. *"No, pardon my manners. You take a sip."* His smile gained in size.

I furrowed my brows in hesitation knowing I could not deny anything I am ever told. I slid the glass back in my direction, slowing pulling it to my lips. A wave of nervousness rushed through my body as the bitterness lay over my pallet. Benjamin motioned for me to down the entire glass. I knew I was in for it seeing as how I was drinking on an empty stomach.

"Pour another."

I did as instructed, sliding it in his direction. Peering inside the glass as if it were contaminated, he asked for another ice cube. Agitation slowly crept its way into my attitude as I plopped in another piece with my bare hand. *"Anything else?"*

Downing the glass with haste, he slammed it down asking for a refill. I tipped the bottle filling it to the line. Unpleased, Benjamin placed two fingers on the neck forcing me to pour until reaching the rim. Dousing his fingers deep into the amber, he pulled out the ice shoving it into his mouth with an annoying suckling sound. *"Drink it."* He firmly pressed his fingertips into the bar top until they whitened.

Taking too long of a pause, two hands pulled me down by the collar leaving my mouth a centimeter away from the glass. *"Quaeram te, ut non!"*

I winced, feeling the cuts on my back burn as healing skin snagged across the fabric of my shirt. Pulling the glass to my lips, I tanked the entirety of dark whiskey down as it battered my throat, tearing a hole in my stomach. Inhaling violently to catch my breath, I felt intoxication driving into my equilibrium the more I attempted to stand upright. Within moments, the room slanted with a blurred haze. Impatient to reach his desired amount of harassment for the day, Benjamin took hold of the bottle slamming it into my chest.

"Drink the entire fucking thing."

I knew my expression read the fact he must have been out of his fucking mind, but I didn't give him the satisfaction. I've had nights where I'd be accompanied by a bottle of Tennessee mash, drinking my worries away until either it was emptied or I had passed out. In the meantime, Ryder called for the meeting to begin.

Benjamin slammed his hands down flat with a reddened face. *"That bottle had better be empty by the time I get back over here. And if you dare to pour any out,*

I will tie you down and shove the bitch down your throat. Understood?"

"Yes, Vice President." My subtle mock partnered up with my next challenge, for the bottle was luckily only half full.

I wanted to pour it out, who wouldn't? In fact, I wanted to smash the fucker over his head hoping to knock his ass into an eternal comatose, but I knew that wasn't an option if I valued my life.

As slick as house mouse, Susurri made her way over to the bar with daring eyes. Standing before me, I had fallen victim to gazing hard into the depth of crystal bathyal irises. Casually running deep red nails through metallic strands of sun kissed hair, the tanned flesh of her petite midriff had me rock solid, yearning to pull her in just to have her against me. To let her feel what it was she does to me without realization.

"I bet you can't…" Her eyes remained fixed on the half empty bottle.

"I accept the challenge." I took a firm grip on the neck, sliding it before me.

Reacquainting my eyes, Susurri deepened her gaze running her tongue across her top lip. My gut ached for her to the point of shriveling up until nothing was left. Placing the opening to my mouth, I tipped my head back chugging as much down as possible.

"Close your eyes…"

I choked up, drooling some onto my shirt. It was then I understood her generosity of coaching me through it. So, I tipped my head back once more and closed my eyes.

"That a lad, keep them shut. With each breath you draw in, pull in the liquid allowing it to flow steadily down your throat. Don't force a swallow or you're bound to choke until regurgitation. Breathe slowly through your nose and soon it will all be over."

Halfway finished, I thought I was going to throw my guts up. But, my taste buds had eventually numbed and wore out against the flavor, leaving my stomach to feel like a sandbag. The bottle sat downward with maybe a drop left inside. I lowered my head hoping to have pleased Susurri with my victory, though I was wrong. Benjamin stood before me, reaching out a hand to whack the bottle from my grasp. Glass smashed to the floor causing everyone to look in my direction.

"Wow, looks like our prospect likes to drink on the job."

I stood fearful with my eyes burning rage, longing to use a shard of glass to cut his fucking throat.

"Even if you scream it, no one will listen. My word will always be taken over yours. Clean up the fucking mess and meet me outside. Nunc!"

Despite my anger, I used my bare hands to pick up the glass, slamming it into the trashcan. I stumbled my way outside falling through the doorway. Benjamin was centering the parking lot, smoking a cigarette. Adjusting his sunglasses, he turned his head to the side exhaling the smoke. I took ahold of a nearby post trying to balance myself when Benjamin flicked his finished butt into the dirt.

"Come on, nequam. Let's have a go."

I felt myself smiling and I wasn't sure if it was because I was heavily intoxicated or the fact of knowing this prick wanted to fight a trained Marine. I stumbled my way down to where he was standing and he threw his fists up ready to fight.

"Why do you want to do this?" I slurred.

"Ha! And the fuck has the nerve to ask why?"

Before I could prepare myself, Benjamin's hand came across my face. The sting shot through my face, but I refused to hit him back. Seeing the irritation in the steel scorn of his face had me shaking my head.

"Fight back, you son of a bitch!"

I shook my head, dodging his next attempt. *"Didn't you learn the first time?"*

"You have some fucking nerve. The first time was irrelevant, because you blindly attacked me. How is that in any case considered fairness?"

"Yet, you challenge me when my ability to protect myself is impossible. You forced me to drink so I'd lose awareness and delude my skills to fight back...ignavus."

Benjamin's expression became still as the breath fell from his mouth. *"Looks like someone has been doing a little research? Don't pride yourself...tu tamen nihil scire."*

I took a hefty step forward daring to enter his personal space. *"I know more than you think."*

"Is that so?" He chuckled. *"Probare gloriantur."*

Grabbing the shoulders of my cut, Benjamin took a forceful knee to my gut sending me to the dirt. I groaned from the pain of my back splitting open. Bouncing around with empty pride, Benjamin dropped down on top of me attempting to get a hit in on my face. I blocked him as much as possible, but the more the alcohol settled in, the more difficult it had become. It took every ounce of strength left in me to keep him off of me as we rolled around continuously in the dirt. Past the point of feeling pain, my body became numb to all sensitivity, so I gave him what he asked for.

"You're no fucking Marine, tu misselus. It's a no wonder why they didn't want you anymore...nequam."

"Vilis!" I spat. *"I am more of a fighter than you will ever be. I am honored and hold more strength than you give me credit for."* I took my left elbow to his jaw

followed by a right hook, watching blood pour from his nose.

Benjamin was persistent with shoving me, trying to push me down—making me infuriated. I hit him, several times over and over, but he wouldn't stop. I could see members standing about, watching the scene. No one moved—no one dared.

"Is this what you want? To give me hell? To hurt me?" I yelled.

Hitting me in the stomach one good time sent me to my knees as I violently threw up everything but my toenails. Taking a hand to the back of my head, Benjamin shoved me over.

"No, it is not what I want. I want you to learn your place. I want you to take responsibility for what you've done!" In a moment of uncertainty, he squatted down beside me flicking open his pocket knife. One in which triggered a memory I longed for disappearance. *"That man you stabbed…he was one of the original founders of this club, he also happened to be our road captain, our brother, and my goddamn uncle!"*

Guilt punched me harder than his fist. Blood and drool dripped from my mouth as I struggled to speak. *"Paenitet…"*

"Fuck your apologies. He is dead because of you!"

"He…he's dead?" I felt sick all over again.

"Died this morning... you hit his aorta. Surgery wasn't enough to help, despite his old age. You don't deserve to be here...for Christ's sake, you don't want to be here. But he did! This was his life and you took it away. Who the fuck are you to portray some higher power?"

I had no words to recover his wounded heart. I never meant to hurt anyone and I hurt each person who was blatantly staring back at me. *"If I could trade places, I would..."*

"And you'd deserve to do so, you bastard!"

I bravely stood to my feet, keeping a safe distance. I could see Adam standing beside Susurri and Ryder in the doorway. Blank expressions painted their faces, no remorse was held for me—it never had been. Understanding the anger and pain I have caused Benjamin to feel was the very reason why he took it out on me. But why allow me to continue to live if he felt so greatly about his uncle?

"I know it means but a damn thing to you, Benjamin. But, I have done things in my life I wish I could take back. I have been forced to do things I didn't want to. Above all, I wish I could take this all back. I really do."

"Yeah...well I hope you live each waking moment in regretful misery." He sneered.

I ran my hands aggressively through my hair following everyone back inside. Ryder took the liberty in beginning the planning stage for a proper funeral. I've attended too many memorial services along with funerals for fallen soldiers and one's who were never found. It never gets easier, especially burying the one's you used to know.

Putting away feelings of grief is a mental anecdote. Your heart caves, but your mind strives to find the willingness to move forward. It finds ideal coping mechanisms, your broken heart beats slowly as your lungs breathe in and breathe out, though you'd rather give up on life if you had the choice. Because, what is life if they are no longer a part of it? Plans become distant memories and those vivid impressions become vague as anger soon rises in their place, leaving you to break down and destroy yourself. Losing someone is never simple; it is always the displacement of the unexpected even if we have estimation.

Death alone is fearless, unstable, unpredictable, and unsympathetic, but is always fierce with its destruction. Its mighty impact has us realize it takes so little to destroy us with an eternity of time to put ourselves back together. If I know one thing better than anything I have learned in my lifetime, it's that life doesn't wait for you and neither does death. We live until we don't anymore. Nothing or no one can prevent that. We find things to fill the space in between waiting in order to keep us sane. If everyone sat around waiting to die, we would never live at all. Pose indestructible

while your heart still beats, just remember…it could
always be worse.

Eight

Running my fragile fingers up the buttons of my shirt, I glared at the reflection of a beaten dog in the mirror. Dressed in black from head to toe, I sneered at the man I was becoming. Each strike that has been placed upon my broken body has all been but a lesson. The more I hurt, the stronger I become. Sliding my shades down to cover my bruised eyes, I could hear my mother ranting around the kitchen. It was unlike her to ever become flustered, so I immediately exited the bathroom to find her.

Waltzing around in frantic distraught, I took her by the arm to regain her attention. *"Momma, what the hell are you doing?"*

"Christ, Rabb. You scared the hell out of me! I thought I told you I needed that window sill fixed, that damn hole is letting wasps in the house and you know I am allergic." She panted.

I couldn't move, I couldn't even register the fact of her calling me by my father's name. My lips quivered as I troubled to speak, it took everything in me to not lose my mind. I figured it was a simple mistake, but I haven't been around much and I have yet to exchange words regarding the doctor visit I volunteered to take her and failed miserably.

Standing with a hand on her hip and the other waving a folded newspaper about had my stomach twisting in knots tighter than a Celtic's.

"Easton...you mean." I said lowly. *"Are you okay?"*

"No, I am certainly not! I have been looking for you for days and you are never around, son. Sorry, my

mind must be boggled due to stress." She sighed exaggeratedly.

"Okay, well calm down and talk to me."

"I am showing signs of memory loss. Doctor says it will only get worse from here. Soon, I probably won't remember a damn thing beyond confusing your name with your father's. It's depressing."

"How long has this been going on? It's not like cancer where it kills you quickly, is it?"

"Easton, I was diagnosed with early onset Alzheimer's. It affects a younger range of people."

"W—what...no? You can't. You're still so young, ma."

"Easton, I am forty-seven years old. It is very possible."

I sat gritting my teeth, tapping my fingertips on the kitchen table. *"What are the symptoms?"* I cleared my throat.

"General memory loss, such as difficulty remembering conversations, names or things I have to do. It can take effect of my physical activity and ability to properly function. I don't want you to worry..." The warmth of her hand slid over mine to calm my jitteriness.

Trying to keep my tears at bay was almost impossible. *"Telling me not to worry again…you have said that once before and now my father is gone."*

"It can take up to eight years before the later stages take over with the severity of the disease. Honey, I have medication and a great doctor. Most importantly, I have you."

"Doctors can only do so much when poor judgment and communication turns into disorientation and confusion when you're lost in the middle of the damn grocery store, momma."

I watched her shoulders sag with an extreme sigh. *"All we can do is take things one day at a time. I was told it is good to continue reading the paper and my novels. Also working in the garden to keep up my physical activity was highly recommended. We will get through this. You're a strong man…the strongest I have ever known. You are my Marine, Easton. Nothing should fear you."*

She was wrong—I was scared to death. Losing my father in an instance was awful, but being forced to sit and watch my mother wither away slowly while forgetting who she is…forgetting everything she's ever known was torture. This must be God's gift of karma for the things I have done. I've killed several of his children…and now I get to endure a large funeral, burying another taken by my hand. If this wasn't hell on earth, then I didn't know what the fuck was.

For the longest, I didn't want to leave the house. But, I also knew I had other business to attend before they showed up on my doorstep unhesitantly. I excused myself before my mother noticed the deep bruising resting in my pigmentation.

Pulling up to the clubhouse, I saw everyone's bikes lined up by rank just the same as the day we rode up to Kentucky. I had shown up a little behind schedule and got hell for it. Lucky me for getting to ride in the back of the line. I shrugged off the unnecessary bullshit and stuck to my purpose.

Members from all over the country were gathered at this ceremony. I became nervous seeing black SUV's with FBI, Homeland Security, local authorities and DEA surrounding the area as if a war were being waged. I minded my own business following my chain of command up towards the front where the podium was located.

Ryder began with a few words to open before Benjamin took over reading off his eulogy. It wasn't until I heard the slightest crackle in his voice as his nose reddened that I witnessed a spark of true emotion and care breaking its way to the surface. I was highly unaware of how appreciated this guy really was; not only to our chapter, but those across the nation. I really fucked up and had no way of fixing it, either.

Thinking I escaped the greatest of detrimental fate...I was certainly wrong. Just as I advanced to head

towards my bike, Benjamin stopped me dead in my
tracks as my name echoed through the microphone.

*"I think you should say a few words of your
own…don't you think?"*

I swallowed hard, turning slowly as a thousand
eyes darted through me. The walk up to the podium felt
like a life time in reaching its destination. I gave a closed
mouth smile while waving a hand.

"If you fuck this up, I promise you will regret it."
He whispered through gritted teeth.

I could see Ryder's eyes enlarge so much that his
eyebrows slightly raised his sunglasses. Crossing his
arms over his chest, his expression looked worrisome.
With Susurri flush to his side, she swiftly ran her
fingers through her hair, gripping a bouquet of white
roses in the other hand.

I drew in a deep breath, puffing my cheeks as my
eyes scanned through the mournful crowd. I had to
treat this the same way I would a funeral for my own,
because these guys were now a part of me.

*"Good afternoon. I'm prospect, Easton Ruckett. I
did not know this gentleman personally. Although, I am
aware of how much he meant to our club, how much he
meant to us as a whole. I regret never shaking hands with
the man who deserved to be here more so than myself. He
is the very reason we have come so far and his legacy
shall not be forgotten, but shall be embraced with every
mile we ride in his name. Eden Ahern was more than just*

another biker proclaimed to be unlawful and unjust, he was our center gravity. A man so historic, it's impossible to ignore his value and contribution soulfully placed within the Disciples. If it were not for him and his creative vision, we would not be gathered here as a unit, today. Each waking moment I am granted with life, I promise to respectfully take responsibility for his absence. I will do my best to fulfill the things he was destined to accomplish beyond his shortened life. I thank you all for showing me what it truly means to be a brotherhood. I used to believe I knew the definition, but I was surly wrong. Hopefully through my future trials, I will find the better part of me and learn to accept it for what it's worth. Until then, I promise to continue full support and dedication to my club as for all chapters across this nation. I pray our brother is not lost, but safe in spiritual preservation. Amen."

Looking through the crowd, my heart sank in my chest seeing Benjamin silently wipe his doleful eyes. What I took from these people was more than I could ever give back. Nothing compares to a life, nothing can balance the wage of a loss of one held so dearly. The fond memory I hold of him will forever haunt me just as the hollow strangers I held captive in my deepest regrets. I felt empty and alone. If these people only knew the truth behind the tragedy, I would not have been securely standing in peace. It'd be my mother standing at the podium struggling to read the lines of forgetfulness. Events no matter how horrific will always change you; it is up to you on how to handle the outcome. I can only ask God to grant me serenity and the strength to keep going, hoping he'd forgive my grand mistakes and lift me while showing me the right way; leading me down the path of righteousness.

The clubhouse was filled with silent screams and hollow stares. Any verbal request thrown my way practically shuttered my insides while I busied myself behind the bar. Ryder was bent over the pool table lining up the perfect winning shot while the dark temptress stood adjacent, eyeing me like I were vulnerable prey in her line of sight. The gleam of cascade eyes beamed in my direction as I refocused my gaze upon the constriction of grip around her pool stick.

The lighting cast a shadow across her pulsing cheek comforting an arched brow of curiosity. I could feel my heartbeat's excessive throbbing send undulation of fire through my veins as my mouth secreted superlative want...no, more like desperate and ubiquitous need.

The dangerous movement of her tongue gliding across her top lip hand my fingers all but tearing apart the bar top as I absentmindedly grinded my groin against the soda gun.

Susurri's eyes darted towards the entrance to the hallway then immediately drove back into mine. I drew in a deep breath while dragging my nails down the firm stubble forming my goatee. She excused herself, vigorously making her way towards the bar. Never leaving my eyes, I watched her seductive strode unapologetically lure me to cautiously follow.

I took a sharp gaze around the preoccupied crowd of members before sneaking off to find her. Entering the dimmed hallway, I spotted the freezer door beginning to close. I cocked my head to the right for a listen—no steps were to be of warning, so I continued on.

Placing my eager hand onto the coolness of the metal handle, a rush of chills soared through my body as my chest tightened; forcing my broadness to suffocate beneath the overbearing fabric. A devious smile pulled my cheeks up in an off-kilter manner as my gaze landed upon black skin tight jeans clinging to the flesh I longed to touch.

The defined taut belly remained sexually pretentious while flawless arms of empowerment clung against the liquor racks with a deadly vice.

Moving in with intolerant hesitance, my lips parted to speak. *"Susurri…"*

"Shh…" She stopped me. *"I see the way you always look at me…and you mustn't, no matter the reason. But the condition granted is one by default because…goddamn it, I love the way your eyes hold me captive."* Susurri sighed.

Dropping her arms, Susurri walked towards me sizing my stature from head to toe. Was it even humanly possible that this woman craved me nearly to the degree in which I did her? Reaching her hand out, I slightly flinched as her index extended towards my face.

But she didn't dare touch my face; instead, she gently ran her index across the back of my cut while she circled around me. I couldn't take her teasing so I snatched her hand as fright filled her eyes. I could only draw my brows together at the thought of confusion.

I turned her hand outward to face her palm up as my other hand trustingly rested upon her waist. *"Touch me…"* I puffed out a rugged breath. *"I know you want to."*

Susurri remained frozen in uncertainty, but the flicker of longing pleasure spoke louder than her timorous actions. I was beyond restraint and patience when I jerked her hand to lay flush against my face. Susurri released a light moan as her breath fell from the angelic lips marked by another man. Bowing her forehead into my chin allowed her scent to travel a forceful wave through my nostrils.

In that moment, I had lost control of my own strength as I forced her back into a corner.

Taking up both of her hands, I placed them against my chest as it heaved boldly beneath. *"You feel that? Susurri…you take the very breath from my lungs each time you enter the room. My chest tightens stronger than the threads that bind a Celtic knot. I want you more than I have ever wanted a damn thing in my whole life and I don't have the right to."* I pressed my cheek down against her neck, slowly dragging its coarseness up the smooth of her flesh. *"Ut mihi tu…"* I whispered.

"Easton…I can't. No matter how badly I want to." She released a wanting sigh.

I took my hands to the back of her ass with a squeeze, pressing her pelvis firmly into mine. With a gasp, Susurri gripped the flaps of my cut, letting the side of her face crash against my chest.

"Do you understand how badly I want you, now?" I groaned.

"If I can only explain the unfamiliar throbbing between my thighs, then yes I concur with your extremity."

Sensing danger, Susurri quickly backed away frantically picking up a full case of beer.

"What's the matter?"

Slamming it into my gut, she swallowed hard. *"Hurry, hold this!"*

Before I could ask 'what for', the cooler's door shoved open. Unable to see who it was as my back remained facing its direction; my heart's pattern took another shock of nervousness.

"Irrumabo, Adam! You scared the hell out of me." Susurri admitted.

"Paenitet. What are you both doing in here?"

I turned to witness a skeptical expression. *"I still am unaware of where everything is. Luckily, she was in here to assist me."* I swallowed hard as his gaze intensified.

Adam and Susurri began having a flustered conversation in Latin with me stuck in the middle. In the center of the crossfire, all I could do was wait. Adam's hand gestures seemed as if he was in doubt with the evidence of our body language as it outshined our false remarks.

Excusing her with irritation, I attempted to follow until Adam's stout chest halted me as the beer case slammed into my own.

"Look me in the fucking eyes right now, Easton. That girl is forbidden! You are asking for danger if you continue this scandalous pursuit."

He noticed my unfazed expression to heed his warning as the clenching of my jaw threatening to crack my teeth before tearing his throat out. Releasing a sigh, Adam gripped my shoulders. *"Is it just sex that you want? If that is the case, you had better go find another tree to piss on, son."*

"I don't want just sex, Adam…" I gritted my teeth.

"She is spoken for. Haven't you ever heard the expression "don't bite the hand that feeds you"? I will not be able to save you from this. I just hope you are at least aware of that."

My eyes drilled a hole straight through him as I gathered my thoughts. *"I guess I will take my chances then."*

"Id malique fati, Easton! You will have a public execution if caught!"

"What will they do, Adam? Hang me?" I jeered.

"Worse. Think of the most horrific thing possible. You think this is a game, but it's not! The advice given is not to ever be spoken of again…if you do this, I advise you to seclude your business in a more private location." He pressed his lips together trying to gain my understanding.

I gave a nod as he took a grip around the back of my neck, playfully shoving me out the doorway.

For hours, I got to endure internal seething while watching Ryder run his dirty hands up and down Susurri's body as she laughed; taunting him…or taunting me. She never did look my way, possibly because I now posed a threat for the both of us. Inside, I could only smile at the fact of getting to finally place my hands on her, breathing her in although it was for a fragment of time. I was going to have her, or at least find a way to tame my inner wolf that howled for a taste of that vulnerable rabbit.

That night, I attempted to please myself using my overbearing imagination before laying my head to rest. My body lied completely exhausted, but my eyes refused to shut all thanks to the midnight ruckus my mother had been causing. I could hear her storming about the house trying to find her sewing kit.

Allowing my erection to become flaccid, I hopped out of bed pulling up a pair of USMC sweatpants over my bare ass. I ran my clammy palms down the perspiration that layered my chest, entering the lighting of the kitchen.

"I swear. Your father loves hiding things from me. Do you happen to know where my basket of yarn is, dear?"

"I think pa might have stored em' up in the attic space. I'll go up and check." I made my way towards the counter top to retrieve the flashlight from the top drawer.

"Easton, you don't have to. It's late."

"Ma, I got it. I'm already halfway there."

I hesitantly made my way up the tiny ceiling ladder trying to find my way around in the darkness. I shone the light over some nearby boxes labeled with *'Rabb's things'*. My throat became dry and itchy the more I neared them. I pulled open the cardboard flaps as old photographs came into view. I took a stack within my grasp to have a better look.

They were of my father's earlier years in the Navy. I passed over a few of him with his fleet and some overseas captures before landing on pictures of us during a cookout. I missed him more than I liked to admit, even though I love my mother just the same; I always found myself favoring my father a little more.

"Easton, did you find it okay?" My mother hollered up the steps.

Glancing over my shoulder, I flashed the light around until I finally found her basket rested on an old cedar chest. Ignoring my deep turmoil of depressive thoughts, I scooped it up making my way back down the steps. The warm smile stretched across my mother's face shot right through my heart as she reached her soft hands up to rub my scruff with gratitude.

"The more facial hair you grow, I swear the more you look like your father. It's a no wonder I get confused from time to time." She joked.

I side smirked at her attempt to seek amusement in her diagnosis. I was absent the final days of my father's life; those men would have to put me down before I accepted to miss those of my mother's. I placed a gentle kiss to her forehead before heading back to my room.

My heart only ached in my chest while I fought to fall asleep.

****

The following morning, only the main board members filled the space of the clubhouse. Falling into my daily routine, Benjamin stopped me; commanding me to come over to the table. I wasn't in the mood for his shit, then again when was I ever?

"What's going on?"

"Sit, nequam." Benjamin shoved me down by the shoulder. *"You'd better stop asking what and why, you bastard."* He backhanded me across the head.

Gritting my teeth until pressure cracked through my skull, I sat reticent while awaiting Ryder's instruction.

"We need to make some money for our upcoming rally. Our chapter got picked to sponsor it this month."

I couldn't be happier to assist rather than be stuck behind the bar, pouring shots for the arrogant imbeciles that drank themselves twelve hours daily into inebriation. What I wasn't prepared for was how we were going to do it. I have never been a fan of organized crime, but having stuck around these guys for nearly a month now—I should've known better.

I had to travel fifty miles north to deliver two kilos to another chapter. I have never dealt with drugs in my entire life and having to personally bring them was beyond my expertise in misconduct.

"Just a little advice, you might want to get you a damn bike of your own. You'll be doing a lot of these from now on."

Breaking my chance to properly respond, a young jackass looking kid walked through the front door. Benjamin hopped up from his seat ready to attack.

"Teneat eam!" Ryder put his hand up. *"You must be lost, young man. Can I help you with something?"*

"I'm looking to prospect for you guys. I have a grandfather who belongs to Kentucky's chapter."

"So what? You come in here demanding some fucking initiation for that? I don't give a shit who your granddaddy is. You're in my clubhouse and you will respect everyone in here. Do you understand?"

He seemed stunned. *"Yes sir."*

"I'll give you some duties around here and we will see how you do. Benny, what do you propose we challenge the boy with?"

A sinister smile twitched at the corners of his mouth as his eyes veered towards me. *"Hey, nequam. This little fucker is now your responsibility. You'd best keep his punk ass out of trouble, because each time he fucks up...so do you."* Benjamin gave him a shove in my direction.

"What's your name for starters?" I asked, trying my best to not show how pissed off I was.

"…Kian" He answered nervously.

"Well, Kian…welcome to hell. One thing to keep in mind, if I get my ass whooped because of your mistakes, I will have your life." I warned.

𝕹𝖎𝖓𝖊

𝕾tanding behind the bar monitoring Kian's ability to fill shots was rather impressive. The kid was a nineteen year old college dropout looking for the wrong turn out for his life. Digging my hand deep into a pilsner, I watched Ryder jump up abruptly from his chair to follow Susurri back towards his office. My instincts twisted in my gut, but I stood motionless only having flashbacks of the accidental time I got to see her fucking mouth lodged full with his damn cock.

"Keep doing what you're doing. I've got to run to the cooler to grab some beer."

I tiptoed down the hallway seeing Ryder's office door barely cracked enough to peer inside. Needing a solid excuse, I went through with the lie I had just told Kian. Grabbing a case of Bud, I made my way back down the hallway to look inside. I nearly dropped the case, letting it shatter once I saw Ryder's hand gripped around Susurri's bottom jaw as she refused to look him in the eyes. I wasn't sure on what they were arguing about, but I wanted to sever his fucking hand off for touching her in such a way.

Dropping my head in dismay, I puffed my cheeks with the great debate on what the fuck to do about it— nothing. I tightened my grip on the handles of the case, yearning to smash it against the wall in the declaration of war. Though, this wasn't my war…my war was no longer overseas, it was my life, my mother and Susurri…I wanted her—God, did I fucking want her. To run my hands up and down every curve of her body, travel my tongue across candied flesh as saliva clung to the fangs hungry to sink inches deep.

Lost in my own daydream, I looked back at Ryder staring directly at me. I looked away while stammering to speak. *"We need to order more Bud Light."* I said dryly.

Planting a firm kiss to Susurri's forehead, I cringed at her squinted eyes locked in a submissive flinch. *"Thank you, Easton. Inform Quaestor or Adam."* He politely nodded just as a cynical gentleman would before closing the door completely.

I drew in a deep breath making my way back behind the bar. Kian was practicing aligning several shots by tossing the small glasses up in one hand, skillfully placing them atop the bar over and over again. I yanked a rag from the shelf, shining bottles and watching with amusement. He wasn't half bad; I guess the kid really wanted to be here. I couldn't understand why, but one might ask why I chose the Corps—because I fucking wanted to, that's why. I guess the same obvious sarcasm would be shared behind an unneeded questionnaire, although one couldn't help but wonder.

As I neatly lined up the freshly glistening bottles in their appropriate place, I caught a glimpse of Susurri in my peripheral. I had to mentally prevent myself from storming over to her demanding to know what the hell happened in that room…but, I couldn't. I disagreed with whatever the issue was that she was forbidden to speak to other men—to me, especially. I refused having further issues with sleeping at night, tossing and turning as my body ached for her.

I am and always will be a man who proudly goes after what it is he wants most. So what do I do? I sit back and patiently wait. But who was I kidding? Those strong defined legs I could almost feel squeezing around my waist as I drove deep inside of her. The clack of heels across the hardwood sent pulsations through my rigidness as my breathing transformed into panting. Shortness of breath always to follow after a single glance had been thrown specifically my way. And now... now I have had her against me, but it wasn't enough. I wanted...no, I needed more. This time was too close for self-control to fail me.

Just knowing how easily unresisting I was to her as she fell against me had me harder than I had ever been. No one has ever had the ability to turn me on so grand...not like that. I was ready to explore further options, though I knew I had to be safe about it. As much as I fathomed the thought of laying her down right there on that pool table and have her for dinner...I knew better.

My thoughts were so intense I could feel my skin burning as sweat dripped down my back and chest. I needed sexual interaction; I was well overdue for a good, hard fuck. But, I was willing to hold out just to relish in every second my appetite was fulfilled with the taste of forbidden fruit.

In the middle of a heated round of poker, Benjamin summoned me over to where he was seated. Quaestor, Chad, and Adam comforted the playing table while Ryder sat back with Susurri tucked into his embrace.

I refocused my attention on the reason why I was standing there to begin with. *"Sic?"*

Benjamin motioned for me to lean downward. *"Walk around the table and tell me if I should fold or not."*

I took a deep breath of annoyance while executing a full 360 degree gander around the entire table. Once I got behind Chad, he stuck out a balled fist pegging me right in the testicles. *"If you so much as help him win, I'll do more than just whip you this time."*

"Someone must have a shitty hand." Benjamin snarked.

Making my way behind Ryder I could see he had a straight hand. Lucky for Benjamin who held a royal flush, he had the right to sit so glee. Witnessing Susurri's hand traveling through chest hair, her eyes didn't dare meet mine. That was only until Benjamin swelled with pride after winning that round, offering for me to play in the next. That gave Kian time to manage the bar a little longer on his own.

I pulled up a chair while Adam shuffled the deck. I had plenty of experience wasting time playing card games while I was overseas. Sometimes, that was our only entertainment despite running away from camel spiders while frantically firing off our 9mm in the middle of a night watch.

A familiar sensation ran down my neck as two arms bowed over my chest while nails dragged up my pecs. I glanced upward to see Moira standing in pure bliss, watching grown men play a foul mouthed game.

"I've watched you since the day they forced your ass to slave behind the bar. I can't help but to want a little piece of our prospect, myself." She giggled.

"Is that so?" I politely smiled.

"No worries there, Easton. She's had a little "piece" of most men walking around here."

"No, more like they've all had a piece of her." Chad corrected.

"Claudere in FUTUO sunt. Like you fellas don't enjoy the vast voluptatem this bitch provides?" Benjamin stated with a swift smack to her ass.

Releasing a squeak, Benjamin pulled Moira down into his lap by her wrist as she laughed, unmoved by the seemingly sensual kisses he placed upon her neck. Her eyes swallowed me; I knew the depths of her want towards me. I just had mine preoccupied—even for her.

Moira was indeed decent eye candy, well at least for a bunch of bikers. I just hated that the one designer piece my mind was set on was shackled to a man I never dared stepping foot to.

Pulling a card from the deck, my attention was captured by the clinking of Benjamin undoing his belt as if he was shameless about everyone watching. Commanding Moira to slide down to her knees, she did as she was told while taking him all the way in. I felt my eyes enlarge as they scanned the table for a similar feeling. But, there was none. Everyone acted as if it was just as ordinary as grabbing the Sunday paper from your fucking driveway after the morning dew had already soaked through the print.

The only one who showed slight disgust was Susurri, but I have seen her in the same position. Even though it was out of public eye, it still twisted my stomach to the point bile rose in my throat at the reminder.

Benjamin left her there until shoving her off when he had had enough. I'm not sure if I was just raised differently, but I would never treat women in the way they did.

"You are leaving at six to make your drop. To make things better, you're taking Kian along for the ride. He has his own bike, don't worry." Ryder informed.

"Sic, sir."

"I see you have been doing a little research on your Latin. How impressive?" Ryder pressed his lips together.

Catching the slightest smirk on Susurri's face had me baring my chops from ear to ear in appreciation. I finished a few more rounds of poker before Adam had me inform Kian of our job. The kid didn't seem too worried about the possible consequences along the way. I figured I could feed off his content mood, but in the back of my mind I still assumed his ass was a bit crazy for not showing the normality of fear.

Standing before Adam's bike, I adjusted my holster before straddling the beast. Adam was busy setting my GPS with our destination. *"Just follow exactly where it takes you. Your product is sealed inside two slip-on exhaust tips that are rested inside Kian's saddlebags. He is your responsibility. If he doesn't make it, neither do you."* Adam glared.

"It says it's only a thirty minute drive."

"And you take advantage of that small increment of time, for it could be your last in this world. Trust me."

I could feel my nerves stabbing with anxiety as Benjamin neared me. *"Listen, you'd better make it back here with the payment, or I'll come find you where you lie. Dead or not, I'll fuck you up."*

"How much money am I to receive? That product is worth around twenty thousand."

"You won't get even close to that. We aren't the fucking mafia. Close enough...but you should get around ten for it. Be lucky we didn't hide the shit in your gut. At least I know you'd be more careful." Benjamin laughed sardonically.

I however, didn't find it comical at all. I just wanted to tear out of the parking lot and never come back.

"See you soon." Adam gripped my shoulder before releasing us.

Kian and I glided down the highway as the sun began to set in the distance. I cautiously glanced down at the GPS throughout our travel hoping not to catch sight of any authority. We reached our destination to a large cabin with AOA above the front doorway.

The rumble of our mufflers drew immediate attention to members standing outside smoking.

Kian stood by his bike hesitantly. *"Do we leave it out here, or walk in with it?"*

"Fuck if I know?" I began heading towards the entrance. *"Let's just get this shit over with."*

Their clubhouse was much livelier than ours usually was. They had twice the women running around cackling about, while members sloshed mugs and argued over treason while playing pool and pinochle. I glanced around the room trying to assemble the identity of their leader when a man with his boots thrown up on a table had caught my eye. I gave a quick suck to my teeth with a snuff, arrogantly adjusting my shoulders as I approached him.

His long hair and John Lennon shades made him pose more down to earth than he really was. *"Can I help you?"*

"I brought something for you."

He raised his head to the left peering behind me and then to my right. *"Did you now? Well, it isn't my birthday. So, whatever the fuck business you have…get to it."*

"I'm prospect Easton…"

"I don't give a fuck who you are." He stood to his feet. Other members crowded in the more irate he became. *"You must think you're something coming in here with your fucking prospect patch stitched on your back. I see you're one of Ryder's boys. Well…he is a close brother. Turn around and lead me to what it is you've brought to me before you piss me off even more."*

I nodded my head for Kian to follow suit. Reaching his bike, Kian began opening his saddlebag.

"No, I want Easton here to retrieve it."

Kian glanced at me without expression as he slowly backed away. Shoving me forward, I became heated. Pulling out two shiny metal slip-ons, they were snatched from my grasp as his watchdogs yanked Kian and I both, forcing us to walk back inside while he opened them in his office. I stood before his desk in parade rest while he disassembled each part. Once getting a look, his eyes met mine in disbelief.

"Is this some kind of joke?"

"Excuse me?"

He called in a member to take a gander and he too looked at us the same. I furrowed my brows in confusion until he curled his finger at me. I stepped forward to see what he was upset about when a dead rat came into view.

"What the fuck?" I jolted back.

""What the fuck" would be an appropriate response."

Slamming me down onto his desktop, a knife was flicked open and kept in my line of sight while he forced me to place my hand down. Spreading my fingers as they trembled within his grasp, he paused with speculation.

"Which finger means the least to you, Easton?"

Sweat ran down my temples until stinging my eyes as his blade pressed into my thumb.

"Let's see, if I take your thumb...you will have an awful time controlling that throttle. I take your trigger finger, you're useless. I can just take your entire fucking hand since you want to mock me."

"I had no idea!" I struggled to move.

His grip on my neck tightened as he moved his blade to my throat. *"I can just cut your fucking vocal chords since you want to lie."*

"What the fuck? He's telling you the damn truth! We were told to bring you cocaine and get money. Hell, it isn't like we are international drug dealers for fuck's sake!" Kian intervened.

"How sweet? Ryder's little bitch boys think they are ballsy enough to run illegal paraphernalia. What they don't know is that we don't run drugs in between clubs. It is not tolerated, what so ever!"

"It's not?"

"Hell no! It's bad enough that we have the fucking DEA and FED's on our asses 24/7. Do you understand the prison time you would do if ever caught?"

He allowed me to stand up and look him in the face. *"Then what the fuck are we doing here?"* I adjusted my shoulders.

He released a slight laugh, shaking his head. I watched him reach into his desk pulling out a stack of money. *"It's what I owe your president. He sent me that rat to be an asshole."* He tossed the stack my way.

"Why didn't he just tell us that to begin with?" Kian asked.

"You sure ask a whole lot of questions. I'm gonna have to speak to Ryder about how he's raising you boys over there. To answer your question, they did it because your naïve and regardless of their reasoning...you were given a job and were expected to do it. You've claimed your payment, so you may now leave before I kick both of your asses for asking so damn much."

Once we hit pavement, Kian laughed his ass off at the fact we were almost dead back there. *"That was intense! How fucking stupid of them to send us off thinking we were dealing some drugs."*

"Well, that may have been true this time. Who knows what else those assholes will make us do. But, I'm quite sure this was a onetime thing."

"Don't be so serious, Easton. Smile a little…Christ—you'd think it'd kill you."

"I am smiling, Kian… on the inside. Let's get outta here."

Standing with his arms folded over his chest as we pulled up, Benjamin wasted no time striding over to snatch the money from my hand. *"So, was Maebeck pleased with his product?"* Benjamin grinned.

"Oh yeah…he was overjoyed."

"Watch your fucking tone. Come inside and have a drink."

I wasn't used to Benjamin offering me a damn thing other than a bloodied nose and busted knuckles, so I strutted right on behind him sharing a thankful smile with Kian.

Everyone inside gave us a proud applause with laughter as we walked through the door. I didn't understand their humor, but I knew I had better get on board and rather quickly at that.

Grunge music waved through the bar as shots of Irish whiskey and bourbon passed through everyone's hands. Susurri and Moira hopped up on the bar, dancing around while pouring liquor down each other's cleavage only to involuntarily tournament me even more. What I wouldn't give just to run my tongue across each mound until all bitterness was undetected.

Looking down at me, Susurri motioned for me to open my mouth as she poured in a long drip of Redbreast deep into my throat. I felt my insides ignite as my eyes watered. My deepened glare cut through her like glass as she tauntingly took in the corner of her bottom lip.

Dragging my fingers through my scalp, my chest heaved as I put a bottle of Ale to my lips. Chugging down until I took in foamed air, I tossed the empty bottle into the trash forcing myself to step outside for some fresh air. The late illuminated flicker of stars and midnight air that flowed through my nostrils had me aggressive and predatorily active. I stared at the moon submissive to its distance just the same as the one between Susurri and I. Even if I were to ever leave this place...she'd never leave my mind.

"Hey kid, you all right?"

I glanced over my shoulder to see Adam approaching as he lit a cigarette.

"I'm good. Just got too hot in there."

"Because of the whiskey...or because of her?" He arched a weary brow.

"I don't believe to know what you're talking about." I smiled.

Adam took a long drag. *"Can I share a similar story with you?"*

"By all means." I posted comfortably against the wall.

"I used to have an eye for this woman they called "Renny", which means small but mighty. And she sure lived up to her name." He smiled. *"Anyway, she had been claimed by some jackass who no longer rides with us for other reasons. I thought I was in love, but infatuation caught up with me and I was relentless when I was younger. I was also given verbal warning to let her be…but I just couldn't."* His eyes hardened with internal pain.

"What did you do about it?"

"Well…the only thing I could. I took her out to this field we used to escape to just to smoke and watch the stars. I made love to her harder than the first day I crashed my bike and hit the asphalt at 70 miles an hour."

"Damn… sounds fierce."

"It's dangerous!" His eyes were still. *"I see the same look in your eyes when you look at Susurri."*

"Were you ever caught?"

"Hell yeah I was! In the worst way possible too—with my fucking pants down." He chuckled. *"It wasn't Ryder who had caught me, that bastard is younger than me and thinks he knows all too well. It was Ardan."*

"The founder?"

"Yep. He didn't physically punish me. For I knew the consequences of what I was doing would be serious. First...he gave me direction to meet him in the office one day and I walked into three other members taking turns on her. Then he hindered me from ever speaking to her again or he'd have my life. When I warned you about public execution, I fucking meant just that."

"What would he have done?"

"Well, he and his partner Eden... they were a powerful duo. They possessed the united power Ryder and Benjamin only wish to claim. Eden was more the aggressor in the club. But, persuasive enough to Ardan...he could make him do just about anything if Ardan believed it was suitable and just. In a nutshell, I would have endured the new age of stigmata."

"Seriously? They would have tortured you and left you for dead?"

"Right there on that post." He pointed. *"This is why I forewarn you about this crush you have going on. I'm a man, too. I understand where your needs lie. Susurri..."* He sighed. *"She's different. More like a special case for Ryder."*

"Special case? How do you mean?"

"If ever possible, I'd rather you hear it from her. It's quite devastating. Hell, it would be for anybody. You seem like a good kid, you were a fucking Marine. I know you know how to obey command of a superior."

"That is totally different. I chose to be a fucking Marine. I didn't choose this!"

"No, your fate did." He corrected.

"Then I guess my fate will choose my path wisely for whatever direction it may lead."

Adam just laughed while putting out his finished cigarette. I tried to sober up by cleaning the bar for an hour or so. I had one too many drinks and was in no condition to ride home on two wheels. Most members had left for the night so Kian and I were left with the mess. I sent him to put away some bottles in the cooler while I stacked chairs to sweep the floor. Singing along with the jukebox, I heard a whisper that caused me to stop. I looked around to spot Susurri leaned up against the bar.

"Come here." She whispered.

I swallowed hard, attempting to take a step forward. The closer I became, the more the broomstick shook within my weakened grasp. Holding a bottle of Jameson in her palm—she grinned devilishly before taking a sip.

"You remember this fantastic formula or torture, do you not?" She licked her lips.

I cleared my throat before choking on my own tongue. *"How could one forced to drink it possibly forget?"*

Kian rounded the corner with his hands shoved deep into his pockets. *"All finished. Everything's put away."*

"If I check, everything will be in its designation?"

"Yes."

"Good. Now get outta here. I'll see you tomorrow."

"Have a good night, Easton and uh…pretty lady?" He laughed.

I awaited the sound of his bike leaving before continuing our conversation.

Taking the broom from my possession, Susurri leaned it beside her before advancing to place her hands on my chest. *"Your breathing…is so rugged, yet shallow."*

"Yes…" I whispered.

"Your heart thrashes beneath a tightened chest…one in which I'm dying to lay eyes upon if you'll let me."

My breath fell from my mouth. *"Let you? ...Give me your hands."*

I took both fragile tiny hands into mine, rubbing the softness of her flesh against the roughness of mine. She watched carefully as I played with each delicate finger before directing them to my buttons. *"Undo them... you have my permission."* My voice lowered.

Her ghostly breath filled the air with a nervous echo as she struggled to undo the top three. The more my chest came into view, the more interested she became. *"I want you to drink this bottle while I examine you."*

"Why can I not witness the sparkle in your eyes as you gaze at my massive chest that longs for your touch?"

"Because, I don't need judgment if I become uncontrollable."

I stared a moment longer before tipping my head back to begin drinking. Soon, I could feel the air hitting my exposed skin as her hands gently pressed against me. A harsh breath escaped my nostrils as whiskey dribbled from my mouth and down my neck.

"I am asking for awful punishment, but damnit I don't give a fuck in this moment."

A warm and wet sensation met my flesh causing my muscles to harden, feeling Susurri travel to my neck leaving a light kiss. I slammed the bottle down on top the bar taking her by the hips to slam her up onto the edge.

"Let me have you." I clenched my jaw.

"Not here…not like this."

"Where is Ryder?"

"Passed out drunk in his office."

I followed her over shoulder glance to reassure myself of no movement lurking about. Reacquainting my eyes, Susurri playfully smiled while pressing a hand into my chest to hop down from the bar. Without stopping, I kept walking backwards until the abruption of a pool table blocking me.

"Lay back."

I inched my way back until laying completely flat on the surface of the entire table. Susurri crawled on top, straddling my waist only to begin ripping my shirt open the rest of the way. I gripped her hips raising mine to press my throbbing erection against her. Gasping, Susurri slammed her palms down into my abdomen, slowly grinding into me.

"You feel that? That... is what you fucking do to me."

"So hard…is it because you desire me so much?"

"…Yes." I felt my lips twitch.

Scooching further down, Susurri took ahold of my belt for a slow unbuckle. My breathing became erratic as she pulled my briefs down, freeing my member to lie against my lower abdomen. Her mouth fell agape at its sight, but she proceeded to place one tiny hand around it.

"My God..." She paused. *"...I want to put you in my mouth."* She released a faint sigh.

Before I could object considering the danger of our location, Susurri already swallowed me down. In reaction, I struck a hand to the back of her head gripping strands of hair, feeling myself enter deeper. The sensation of her teeth sent a wave of tremors throughout my body as her jaw constricted around me. I was almost in shock at how good it felt that I could hardly keep control. Sucking at me harder and harder, I raised my hips thrusting deeper to feel the back of her throat.

"If I can't be inside you, let me fuck that pretty little mouth of yours." I groaned.

Susurri moaned against me taking, all of me in. I couldn't stop...I wouldn't until I reached my release. Right before I hit my peak, her eyes landed straight on mine, digging her nails deep into my abs as I pumped my release down her throat. I couldn't move—my orgasm's intensity had me frozen against the table. Susurri took it as a compliment by assisting me with fastening my jeans.

"That was amazing." I exhaled.

Susurri's cheeks reddened as she slid to her feet. *"I wanted to make you feel as good as I do every time you look at me. That's how I feel inside."*

"I was unaware on how just a simple look could cause one to buckle at the knees."

"Because, when you look at me… you see me. And that alone makes me feel beautiful, if not sexy at times."

"You deserve to always feel what you are—beautiful."

"You'd be surprised on how I've felt in my life."

"Let me ask you this, what is Ryder to you?"

She ran her hands through her hair before reaching into her back pocket. A lighter and twisted paper came into view. Igniting its tip, smoke soon flowed into the air.

"I need to calm my nerves to get into that. Do you want some?"

"I've never smoked a day in my life. I wouldn't know how." I admitted.

"Oh, I forgot…Mr. Marine." She giggled. *"Just try some, you may like it. It's not horrible, Easton."* I stood up with a shrug as Susurri placed it in between my lips. *"Now inhale."*

I felt dense smoke enter my lungs as I coughed several times. After the third hit I was feeling unlike I ever have before. I felt weightless as I gazed harder into Susurri's eyes as she spoke.

"I have lost both parents…" She began. *"I remember it all as if it were yesterday. My mother and I waited for my father to come home from work so we could go walking down the highway where the sweetest strawberry field was found. Daddy hated paying the price for them at the market, so instead he'd take me and momma down the road to pick some just for us. One day he came home in a rather unfortunate mood. I remember it being work related, but as soon as he saw my depressive eyes he gave in and took me and momma on our traditional walk."* She smiled to herself. *"I was in the middle, tightly secured by each of their hands as they counted to three and swung me in the air over and over just to hear my childish giggle. They placed me down as we reached the field but a bailer truck was hauling down the road behind us. I can still see the fear in my father's eyes as he screamed to get me out of the way. I guess the driver had been doing some drinking and swerved off the road."* Horror filled her eyes as they glazed over. *"My father yanked me up tossing me at least three feet from the ground to safety by the time the truck reached us. I screamed…I screamed so loud seeing them both lying there helplessly…painted red and motionless. I tried waking them up, yelling to hear a response, anything. But nothing came. That was the last time I ever went to that field and I haven't eaten strawberries since. And to think*

I was only six years old when that happened. Can you believe how cruel life is?"

The gloss in her eyes had my heart ache for such a tragic loss.

"Yes, I can believe it." A frown challenged my face. *"After that?"*

"Then, after lying helplessly for hours crying over my deceased parents, a loud roar in the far distance caused me to jump up. I was thankful to have any human contact at that point, I didn't care who it was. Well, it ended up being a group of Disciples with Ardan in the lead. He ended up taking me in and raised me as if I were his own."

"So, when did Ryder take the throne?"

"About four years ago after Ardan died from natural causes. God, he was so damn old. He claimed I had given him the wisdom to remain living for all those years. I still remember how faded his tattoos became, as if they were dark birthmarks." Susurri sat in slight nostalgia.

"How old was he?"

"Eighty one. But, Ryder on the other hand is Ardan's first born son. He claimed position by default. Yes, we have an age difference and you would think we were like brother and sister. But, that wasn't the case. Ryder was not allowed to interact with me as a child. Ardan didn't want me becoming a part of this lifestyle,

but it had become all I knew. As I became an adult things soon changed. Ardan gave me the choice to live freely and forge my own path, but this is what I chose instead."

"At first, I couldn't understand why the hell anyone would want to be a part of something like this. I guess it makes more sense now. I am so sorry for your loss though, I lost my father three years ago to a massive heart attack. I actually know loss far beyond my father, but I hate talking about it." I looked down at the floor. *"Not even my best friend Draper, nor my mother dares to ever ask me about it."*

"You know loss and you know war probably more than you've ever wanted to experience. It sucks when things are out of your control. That's why I smoke or occasionally take a Xanax. I used to be so badly addicted because... I loved the feeling." She zoned.

"What did you feel?"

"Numb. It was my escape from the world. I didn't have to deal with anyone or anything—it was just me and them. The only time I was happy was when I was high. It scared Ardan to death to see me like that—morbidly pale and thin. I would look at myself in the mirror disgusted and confused at how something living could appear so dead. Ardan made Ryder promise to look after me...and he has done just that."

"Then what draws you to me?"

Her eyes drove into mine. *"Ryder is the only man I've known outside of a father figure. The only one I have ever felt love and protection with. Then you came into my life and I could tell from the first look that I wanted to know more…but I wanted to know more with you."*

Ten

𝕴 sat spaced out on the porch, absentmindedly dappling a teabag into hot water. I couldn't get Susurri off my mind and the duration of waiting for Draper to arrive felt like an eternity. I drew in a honey scented breeze looking towards the garden in which consumed my mother. I was intrigued with how easily crouched down she was, sprucing dirt around freshly planted bulbs, delicately smoothing her gloved fingers over silk pedals. It brought her peace and tranquility, I could tell by her smile and relaxed posture each time she began a new project. Then the instance of her having the right to sustain her own freedom to enjoy such simplicity in life soured my stomach knowing that not everyone had that privilege.

The rumble of Draper's old beat up GTO his father passed down after graduation came rolling through the drive. I wetted my lips before taking a sip of chamomile as his boots clacked up the porch steps.

"Howdy." He tipped his black pinchfront cowboy hat with a casual smile.

"Good morning."

"Your mother called me the other day and told me you guys had a discussion about her medical issues."

I rolled my head side to side, cracking my neck with slight irritation. *"Yep, sure did."* I took another exaggerated sip.

"Look, she made me promise not to tell you while you were over there. She claimed your Sergeant didn't think it was a good idea because it would cause you unnecessary stress. I even tried writing it in a letter once, but I knew you'd be unable to handle it because Rabb had recently passed..."

"I know what the fuck it would have caused, Draper!" I bit out. *"And you're right, I wouldn't have…"* My eyes locked on his submissive expression. I took a hard swallow, fighting back a much needed breakdown. *"You don't know what it was like over there…I wouldn't want you to. Having a death in the family isn't the same as seeing them die before your eyes—especially so violently. Imagine someone you've trained with and you both had become brother like. You both swear on each other's life to be battle buddies no matter what."*

"Did…did you lose someone, Easton?" Draper was hesitant.

Memories of the craziest moments I shared with that kid flashed through my mind as my face flushed with the hurt uprising beneath my chest. I felt my lips quiver as the force field of indestructible egotism allowed a tear to escape down my cheek. *"Yeah, I did."*

"You don't have to tell me anything more."

"No…no, I want to. I need to before I lose my goddamn sanity." I puffed out a rugged breath. *"Sergeant Ballintino and I were close from the moment we met in boot camp. He had the rack next to mine. I remember nights we'd piss other recruits off from staying up late, just throwing the bull. We didn't give a shit, which is why we got stuck doing fire watch every damn week."* I gave a light chuckle. *"He was this 5'4" Latino, but he was stalky and strong as hell. Anyway, I found out we shared the same MOS and went to training school together. I think there was only one assignment he had*

that we weren't stationed together and that was when he had gone to Japan. I didn't see him for almost two years. We ended up getting deployed together twice."

"What was your job?"

"MOS-0311. We were the primary infantry position in the Corps. We were rifleman." I smirked with pride.

Draper's eyes widened with impressiveness. *"Oh yeah, how could I forget those stories about how you two used to pull chicks at almost every bar for wearing your damn uniforms."*

"Yeah, that guy. We were out on a scout when we entered an open range. The eeriness of it still gives me the chills till this day. Ballintino didn't have a care in the world in that very last moment he could ever smile. Well, I thought I saw movement up ahead inside a rundown building. Raising my M27, I aimed in its direction. Ballintino raised his hand to halt my movement when I asked if he had seen it too. He just nodded, counted down from five on his fingers before continuing onward. I didn't feel right, so over my headset I requested our back up to move in faster just in case something happened. Looking through a pair of my binoculars, I could have sworn to see the tip of a rifle. As other Marines moved in, Ballintino turned around giving a confident chuckle telling me it was all right and that nothing could overpower the strength of our unit. Suddenly, Arabs appeared through the opening of windows high up, I was in complete shock that I couldn't tell him "turn around,

look!" before getting sprayed in the face with my best friends blood. The reality of him being dead didn't settle in just yet. The other Marines from our unit joined me in a shoot off until taking cover back over a fucking hill. I dragged Ballintino's body for nearly a mile, screaming that I wasn't going to leave him and that we were almost to safety. I trucked so hard through deep sand, securing my rifle into my chest nearly feeling the tendons in my left arm tear. Once I saw his lifelessness lying next to me, I blacked out. It's all a blur from there. I know I have blocked a lot of it out since, but standing at that man's memorial service was greater than the impossible. He had such big dreams, such high expectations for himself…but at the same time he loved life. He was truly fearless and I envied him for that. There isn't a day that passes that I don't think about him. I occasionally hear from his mother, but it's been a while since the last time we'd spoken. I'll never forget the sadness in his parent's eye. Even the girl who had his heart was mortified into muteness. I had witnessed death a few times before that day, but it never affected me in the way Ballintino's had. He had me so convinced that he was invincible and then I realized no one really was, they just get fucking lucky. Even the most cautious of mankind die from tragedy."

Draper was in bewilderment; as if he wished he had never opened his fucking mouth to begin with. It was all right by me, I needed to unleash my entangled emotions. The only person I ever repeat it to was my damn self.

I didn't want sympathy or sorrow; I just wanted

to erase my memory of ever knowing him; it hurt so damn bad. A girl I had relations with back in California couldn't break through to me afterwards. I actually believed I was going to marry her, but after losing my other half I didn't want to become close to anyone else.

Sex wasn't sex, she told me it was like looking into the eyes of a soulless man—that I wasn't there anymore. And when I was in a participating mood, I'd fuck her so hard just to release anger and shed the survivor's guilt. She'd stay up some nights crying over the nightmares I suffered and the loss of love I left back in that open range.

Then I think about the desperate need of affection I have gained for Susurri. It wasn't because I was lonely and obtained relentless urgency...it's because for the first time in three years, I could actually feel something again. It has been months since I have shared any type of sexual contact with another woman. Yes the drought has been one of difficulty, but waiting for so long has made me appreciate any opportunity when it prevails.

Long after Draper left, I sat in my room thinking of a way I could get away with murder. The fact I had been recently avid on learning to how speak and understand Latin, I wrote a simple note on a bar napkin, awaiting another for opportunity to appear.

All evening, I kept making eye contact with Susurri while the board discussed business over the meeting. Since Kian has tagged along, I have actually earned the right to attend these fucking meetings. Ryder was going over our monthly dues we owed; I went to drop a fifty in the bowl when Kian came up from behind whispering a rant about how he didn't feel he should have to pay that amount.

Overhearing our conversation, Benjamin threw his chair back, jumping up to his feet. Everyone stopped what they were doing just to watch.

"What the fuck makes you think you don't have to pay?"

"He meant he shouldn't have to when he has a friend like me to pay for him." I bit out while pulling another fifty from my wallet.

My eyes never left Kian's until Benjamin grabbed me by the flaps of my cut to slam me onto the table. *"Well, aren't you just the sweetest, nequam? But it isn't up to you. Everyone pays their own fucking dues! If you are having an issue with that then you had better tell either Ryder, or me."*

"Benjamin, have him go out and clean everyone's bike." Chad laughed.

An evil grin stretched across Ryder's face. *"I have an even better idea."*

Stripped down to our boxer briefs, Kian and I were tied together through our legs and around our wrists so movement without either tripping or giving unwanted friction to our balls was impossible. Other members hounded and taunted us for hours for their own enjoyment. I could have whipped Kian's ass for the cause of extreme embarrassment.

By sundown we both wore raw hides and enough insults to last us through the next lifetime. Ryder stood up by the doorway with Susurri's back pressed into him as he rubbed up and down her hips. I disguised a snarl as Benjamin stalked up with a switchblade to cut us free.

"Hmm…hey, Chad… I think Kian missed a spot on your muffler."

"Did he?" Chad asked, heading straight for us. *"Give me that."* He snatched the switchblade pointing it at my face. *"Give me your wrists."*

I raised them as we made eye contact. Looking at my fearless reflection through his pupils, my chest twitched as the blade slid clean through the rope.

"Go the fuck on!" He shoved me over.

Benjamin slammed my clothing into my chest before walking away. *"If you think for one second to intervene here in the next sixty, I swear to God I'll cut your dick off so it never feels the pleasure of a tight cunt again!"*

I cut my eyes as his back turned. The seriousness of the club's change in attitude had me alert as I struggled to get my jeans pulled up. Both Chad and Benjamin exchanged words in Latin. I could hardly make out everything due to their quickness of slang. At first, Kian looked unworried while waiting to be released.

"Incumbam…" Chad said dominantly.

"What?"

"He said bend over, damnit!"

Benjamin took Kian by the back of the neck, throwing his bound wrists around the sissybar of Chad's bike. I yanked my shirt over my head hurrying to slide my boots back on as they ripped the knife through Kian's briefs until they fell to his feet. I was uncertain on what the fuck I was about to witness, but I didn't like where things were leading. I felt my feet absentmindedly begin to lure me in their direction as Chad undid the front of his jeans. There was no way in hell they were planning on publically raping the kid—I mean, would they?

Feeling me gain in proximity, Benjamin yanked out his .357, pointing it right at my chest. *"Step propius and I'll kill you both."*

I took a minor step backwards while glancing over my shoulder. Ryder showed no expression and beneath her shades, Susurri's face remained stone. Watching Kian jerk about screaming for mercy, I could only look away trying to block out the sound. No one moved to help him; no one gave a fuck because this was their way of life. If you make a mistake, the punishment is always soon after.

Their way of control was to fuck you up and manipulate your mind into believing they were your superiors, your life is theirs and if you can't handle it then you need to get the fuck out. The more things like this happened, the more fear was drilled into my gut at any thought of touching Susurri. If they tormented Kian over not paying his dues, what the fuck would they do to me if I were ever caught fornicating with Ryder's ol' girl? Just the stories Adam had told me didn't seem so real until witnessing such a thing in person.

The world seemed to slow as Adam handed me my cut while pushing me to go inside the clubhouse. He wasn't pleased with how things have been going these past few years and he released years of pent up anger and disgust on me.

"Do you see what I mean, Easton?" He paced back and forth.

I slid on my cut, fastening the button extenders while he gathered his thoughts.

"Things have changed since Ardan died. They are fucking animals! It isn't about riding and representing what it means to be a true American badass. It's about money, power and control. If you disobey their word, you better pray to whatever higher belief to fucking save you 'cause no one here is sure as hell going to do it!"

"Adam, they want people to fear them. How else can you make that a possibility if you never prove to

*people you are the baddest and that you are the worst
thing since the creation of empowerment."*

*"People do fear us. They are going to make that
kid a monster after what they had just done. The ones to
fear the most are the prospects who haven't earned the
right to wear a 1%er patch. They are blood thirsty just to
prove their dedication and loyalty to the club. I have seen
some of these guys do some outrageous things. What the
fuck do you think they will do to you…you can't exclude
her from the equation. You will put her in for the worst
consequences and they will make you suffer."*

*"No! Fuck that! They don't own me and they sure
as hell don't own you!"*

*"What do you not understand about how
organized and powerful these guys really are? That could
have easily been you out there. Luckily, right now it's
only your fucking mind that has put its dick inside her."*

I was flustered. I didn't want to fucking hear
anymore, but Adam was determined to make me see to
understand.

*"You know what? Come here and look over by the
last post. Tell me what you see."*

I glanced through a group of females down at the
end, smoking cigarettes while talking to one another.
"Property victims having a smoke?" I shrugged.

*"You see the short one with really long dark hair
pulled back in a perfect braid? That is Renny."*

Feeling our gaze, her eyes glanced in our direction and I never knew how loud a conversation could be just through the eyes. How would I feel if all I could do was pass my feelings and thoughts through eye contact? They were truly the windows to the soul. I wouldn't have been able to hang around and continue to torture myself.

"Why don't you just leave then?"

"Because, I didn't dedicate thirty years of my goddamn life to this club and have it all have been for nothing!"

"This isn't living? This is a damn Nazi camp ran by circus monkeys!"

To interrupt our conversation, a loud commotion came stumbling inside the clubhouse. Benjamin had Kian by the back of the neck, shoving him inside to go clean up in the bathroom.

Nausea stung my stomach at the sight of his crippled posture as he shook traumatically. I immediately made my way behind the bar busying myself before I went on a psychotic rampage. The familiar sound of heels clacking against hardwood raised my eyes. Susurri walked by with Moira, but catching me in her view they both stopped.

"Give me a shot of Kilbeggan."

"Yes ma'am."

"It's too pathetic how there stands a perfectly masculine gentleman, yet she wouldn't know how to handle a man such as your stature." Moira scoffed.

Pushing the shot in her direction, I read the embarrassment upon Susurri's face. *"I'm not quite sure I know what you mean by that?"*

Downing her shot seductively licking her lips, Moira gave a sarcastic laugh. *"Because, I have experience."*

"That much I have seen for myself." I replied casually noticing a smile tug at Susurri's cheeks.

Walking around the bar to stand inches away, Moira gently placed a hand on my bulge with a whisper. *"She may have sucked your cock, Easton. But, I doubt she'll ever spread her legs for you."*

My breath caught up in my throat as my eyes landed back on Susurri. Moira placed a light kiss of death onto my grainy face before strutting away.

"Pst…Susurri, wait!" I whispered.

She stopped instantly, but didn't turn to look at me. Sliding the napkin across the bar top unnoticeably, I barely connected our fingertips. *"Please…think about it?"*

For days, Susurri didn't speak to me after receiving the note. I couldn't come up with a reason why. Maybe I was too forward; maybe she's afraid of what it could cost. I was never one to break the rules, but what is beauty without rage? What is passion without fear? What is love without struggle? What would life be without drawing in the very breath she gives you? –Consequence.

Eleven

Flying down the highway in a tightknit formation, I felt a different kind of freedom gliding on wheels instead of marching in lockstep by foot. No flak jacket, Kevlar or rucksack to weigh me down. It was me and the world around me as I took control of the winding road beneath anxious tires.

We parked in a perfect row to announce a grand arrival in the pine scented air of North Carolina. I arched my back for a nice stretch to bring life and motion back into my legs and ass. This rally was much larger than the one back in Kentucky. This time it was only members from fellow chapters in the nearby area. I actually felt a sense of security being around supposed family members.

Relentless and unnerving as always, Moira waltzed up to me looping her arm within mine; delving into a want for my life story. I didn't give her much attention for my being screamed apathy once my eyes landed on the petite leather jacket formally fit to defined curves. Tight blue jeans clung perfectly around heeled boots, her hair neatly pinned back with a blackened bandana while hiding her eyes behind infamous sun shades. The gleam of polished nails bared advertisement as she reached her hand out to receive a cup of draft. Without realization, I neared with shallow breathing only to choke seeing Ryder's hand run over her ass.

Smiling at the tender, Ryder dug his fingers into her back pocket while grabbing his drink with the other hand. Susurri looked up at him with a smile as he pulled her in tighter, placing undeserving lips atop her little forehead. My head ached from the clenching pressure of my jaw as I stepped closer.

"Do you want a drink?"

Moira side smirked with delight. *"What a gentleman? Yes, of course."*

Her pleasant attitude was so overbearing with bitchiness it had caused Susurri to look over her shoulder. I kept a still posture with an unwavering gaze watching her lips part with surprise. Motionless, we shared an intimate moment through silence before the arching of an envious brow lurked above black frames as Susurri caught view of Moira attached at my hip. Wetting her lips with class, Susurri pulled Ryder in closer as he intensified his squeeze making her squeak. He gave a deep subtle laugh hauling her away into the crowd. I couldn't break away my stare until they were both completely out of sight.

"What's up, fucker?"

Moira and I turned simultaneously to see Chad standing with Benjamin and Kian close behind. The kid looked different, not just in his apparel—but in his face as well. Despite a busted lip in healing, his eyes were dark and demon like. Reaching to take ahold of my beer bottle, I felt a swift kick land on the back of my left knee. Being a Marine, I knew better than to lock them up, so I didn't fall with his attempt.

"Here, hold these." I told Moira.

Turning around to see their offensive expressions didn't bend me enough to cause commotion.

"Oh, I forgot. Gravissimos, potest de defendere." Chad jeered.

Benjamin reached forward grabbing ahold of my cut, but I stood unreacted.

"Someone has some big balls because the "Ide of Medb" is digging her poisonous talons into the nonnative flesh. Just ask her how much she has taken at once. I bet your little prick wouldn't feel a damn thing but empty space." Benjamin laughed. *"She's a scortum with amara pussy."*

"O, te ipsum! If I remember correctly, numquam quererrentur." Moira spat.

Just like that, Benjamin back handed her across the face. *"You ungrateful bitch! How dare you speak to me in that way?"* Out of anger he struck his hand around her throat, pulling her face into his. *"If I remember correctly, I was the first to please that wet cunt of yours."* He bit out. *"I showed you the ropes...breaking that back in each time I had you on all four."*

I didn't open my mouth and I sure as hell didn't intervene. Chad may stand an arrogant prick, but he is quick to remind you of your place against his and just how powerless you found yourself afterwards. I knew she didn't deserve the public humiliation from innocent standbys, but she wasn't my bitch—therefore, she wasn't my responsibility.

Benjamin released her with a shove before snatching her beer to chug it. Nearing her personal space, Benjamin smashed the empty bottle into the trashcan before aggressively pulling Moira in by her ass. *"I am and always will be primum when it concerns you."*

Leaving us to ourselves, Moira glared at me with disappointment. *"Well, how the hell are you to just stand by watching that happen?"*

"Do you honestly think I'd get my ass kicked over you?"

Moira jerked her face to reacquaint my eyes; peeved. *"But, you'd get whipped just to prove your ego against another man's? I saw where your eyes locked during the duration of your well-deserved punishment."*

"You sure have a filthy mouth considering where it's been."

"You bastard! You wouldn't dare say such things with Benjamin and Chad standing here...but you will disrespect a woman so easily as if she's beneath you."

"You are not and never will be above me. You have no class, no shame, and lack self-respect as a fucking woman. It isn't disrespect if I am speaking the truth."

"You don't know a goddamn thing about me, where I come from, or what the hell I've been through. At least I am not chasing after lost hope."

"What the fuck does that mean?" I stood taken aback.

With a charismatic smile, Moira took the beer from my grasp taking a small swig. *"It means you can have me or anyone else. I promise you that you will never have her in this lifetime and surely not the next, either."* Chugging the remaining contents from the bottle, Moira effortlessly dropped it into the trashcan before walking off.

Finding myself lonely momentarily, I bought two more bottles for the purpose of chugging both until Adam ran into me.

"Damn, from afar it looked as if you and Moira were having a romantic conversation." He grinned.

"Yep, sure was." I smiled back while offering him a bottle.

Leaning our backs against a tree, Adam and I both sipped on our beers while people watching. He didn't have much to say furthering a conversation he knew the outcome of.

I needed to know where the fuck Moira was getting all of her little details of destruction from. I had to keep things pleasantly mild with the woman who could easily slip a wicked tongue into the ears of the ones who claimed my life. Even if a little apologetic drunk fuck had to take place, I'd do whatever the cost just to keep her fucking mouth shut.

Walking through the crowd, I could feel the shots of Crown overtaking my inhibition as Adam stood offering me another. I waved him away trying not to upset my balance.

"I am way too fucked up right now, Adam."

"Look at those barbaric heathens." He pointed.

My attention turned towards Chad and Benjamin taunting two members from another chapter in a circle fight. In slow motion, I watched them throw fists as blood dripped with each contact made. Ripping their shirts off revealing skin covered in testosterone and egotistical vanity; the crowd riled them up with a clamor for more. I stumbled forward with an inviting laugh, falling into the people in front of me.

Pressing a firm boot down to catch my balance, I could feel another foot beneath mine. Causing the man pain, he shoved me by the face telling me to fuck off.

Landing straight into the middle of their playtime, Benjamin stopped everyone while walking over to me. *"Get the fuck up, nequam!"* He kicked me in the stomach.

I doubled over wincing with extreme pain. Rolling onto my hands and knees, Benjamin pulled me up by the shirt collar with impatience. *"I said get up! Kian, get your ass over here, now!"*

Chad gave him a dramatic push as he toppled over before me. Through blurred vision, I squinted to gather reality around me. Moira stood behind another female with her arms crossed over her heaving chest.

"I want you to entertain us."

"How?" Kian asked.

Running at full speed, Benjamin leaped from the ground sending a death punch straight to his face. *"Like that...you want to ask another goddamn question?"*

Pulling out their switchblades, Kian and I were forced to entertain the harshest of men around us. Scorns ran deep with regretful history of once being in our position. But, we must learn our lesson right? We mustn't forget our place.

I bent down to offer a helping hand when Kian grabbed my hand in the same way Ballintino used to every time I ever had to help his drunken ass up, or after a tiresome match of MCMAP, even after too long of a nap on a pile of sandbags in 120 degree weather before our shift began.

At first, I was upset looking into the eyes of someone I missed so dearly, then anger rose as I yanked him up with a loud scream. I repeated in my head over and over again that I always do what I must to survive and this was a moment unchosen like any other I had endured. Kian looked scared until I gave him a shove just to provoke his inner fighter. He knew just as well as I did what would happen if we refused to do as instructed.

Throwing a hefty punch to my jaw, I nearly blacked out with its force. Blood poured from my mouth after my back teeth clamped down onto the inside of my cheek. All I could do was laugh as it rolled down my chin. The vociferation of everyone around us only angered me more as Kian's fist had met my nose. Even more blood began pouring down my face and onto my chest.

Drawing in the sight of Susurri standing with Ryder and Moira, I froze. I had to regain my senses before I let my ass get handed to me by this punk ass kid. So instead of taking another quick shot to my face, I ran at Kian's waist, lifting him up into the air just to slam him back down. I hit him over and over, enjoying his fight to get me off.

This was my moment to feel in power, to feel the control of a fucking situation even if I couldn't stop it. My knuckles bruised beneath the surface as Kian's blood stained their tops. After taking one too many hits, Kian's eyes began rolling into the back of his head. Blacking out and losing control, I felt arms go underneath mine to lift me off before I killed him.

I was angry and embarrassed at the pride and glory thrown my way from the crowd's applause. Adam was the one who saved me from losing myself. Catching sight of Benjamin doubled over; laughing as if he won me over only angered me all the more. Drunk and disorderly, I staggered my way to an inside bar in search of a bathroom.

Standing before the mirror, freshly painted in crimson, I scooped cold water onto my face cringing from the pain settling in. As I watched clouded water swirl down the drain, the door opened in my peripheral. The perfect escape stood in reflection with me. Watching Moira part her lips to release an asinine remark, I quickly turned and grabbed her by the throat while covering her mouth.

"Shut the fuck up."

Her eyes widened with surprise as I hoisted her onto the counter top, yanking down her jean shorts. She immediately magnetized her hands to my belt, ripping my zipper as I glanced down at tanned legs with a glistening invitation. Growing in ossification, I shoved myself inside, slamming into her unexpected tightness over and over again. I didn't want affection from this, I wanted satisfaction. I wanted to fuck my pain and anger away before I lost my fucking mind. Moira bit her lip moaning loudly in my ear as her legs clenched around my hips. Unable to stabilize my intensity, Moira attempted to latch onto my chest with her nails.

"Don't touch me and don't you dare put your lips on me. You just fucking sit there just like that and let me finish." I bit out.

Without an argument, Moira gave a nod while planting her hands down onto the counter with a deep arching of her back. Maybe she had done horrible things in her past, but so have I? It wasn't right to judge her and I knew inside I was wrong for my assumptions. The way she enjoyed me ramming into her moist tissue layered my erection as it shined in the lighting with each visible stroke.

At first, I lost myself in my own thoughts and then it actually began to feel good. All I could think about at that point was coming all over that tight stomach baring silver jewelry. The faster I went, the louder she became and I actually liked it. I wanted more reassurance that I was the reason she was feeling so good. Even with a decent amount of experience, if a man hasn't released in a while... he may very well lack in resistance.

Falling into her own comfort of pleasure, Moira bit her bottom lip trying to control herself as she reached back towards the mirror for stability. She became louder and louder with time and nearly lost her own fight to keep her hands off of me.

Somehow, Moira constricted her muscles around me with pulsation as if she were trying to pull me in further; we both looked down watching me drive in slowly. A sharp pain stabbed my lower abdomen hearing the echo of my groan as I struggled to hold out. Tightening around me, I pulled back exploding all over her stomach. I have never fucked a woman who claimed such muscle control and it felt amazing.

I took a moment to adjust my breathing, feeling Moira staring into me. I jerked my belt to fasten it while grabbing a handful of paper towels. *"Here, clean yourself up."*

Still lightly panting with a deadly glare, Moira responded. *"Nothing beats experience."* She scoffed.

I lurched forward with dominance while gripping her thighs. *"But, I felt you cum at least twice as you clinched around my cock, darling."* I shot a wink, giving a self-assertive grin before exiting the bathroom.

I stumbled my way back out into the sunlight to find Adam. He was leaned up against a nearby post taking a snooze—probably having to sober up. I could see other bikers going round after round in matches of decimation. I didn't think I could keep going on like this, or to ever become accustomed to this type of lifestyle. There hasn't been a day that has gone by that I didn't wish I never set foot in that fucking bar that night. Even if I had stayed in for a third enlistment, I would have been no good to my unit. My medical chit regarding my loss of mentality can even concur with the fact.

Watching Moira slither through the crowd, standing in my line of sight had me disgusted with myself. I know while stationed overseas I have had my fair share of one night stands and moments I can't remember, ever after waking up next to someone else. But, how I approached Moira was out of my own ways. Or maybe the ways I am setting are the ones taking over to create the man I need to be in order to survive out here.

Twelve

Waking to bright sunrays beaming against my face, I cracked my eyes open bringing the room into focus. I overslept, but my body surely needed the extra timeout. I gave a light trim to the hairs of my goatee, ignoring the brushed stubble on my cheeks. Dropping my eyes to gaze at my chest, my mind opened a memory portal causing a reminder of how good it felt when Susurri placed her hands against it. Even through a subtle encounter, I felt a strong connection and I knew she did as well. My muscles twitched at the thought of how badly I desired to taste her as my delusive thoughts unraveled.

Ceasing the porcelain sink within my titan grip, I pressed my head against the mirror in a moment of self-reassessment. If Susurri didn't so much as look my way today, I just might tear the shelving from the wall.

My mother was rested on the couch with a Dutch Trowel in her clutch. Leaning against the doorway, I began to emanate my feelings while I watched her sleep. The sad part was I have never been voluntarily open with her and I knew she was unfavorable over the fact.

"Ma, look at you so peaceful…" I released a heavy sigh. *"…a feeling I have forgotten years ago. I know you never ask about my years of service, though I fought from telling you over each phone call we ever had while I was away. Some nights, I'd struggle to speak trying my hardest to keep from crying. Not just because I missed you, but because I also missed pa…and I missed being home. Over there was never peaceful, it was never happy. I was in someone else's home, hurting their families while trying to protect my homeland brothers."* I paused with a snivel. *"I know I haven't been around like I should have, but I want you to know I am okay. I am just dealing with life and its deranged consequences.*

Even if I tried explaining everything to you, it wouldn't matter none… because someday you won't even remember who I am." I began lightly sobbing. *"I haven't forgotten what you've been battling, not even the sadness in your eyes the day we spoke about it. I showed anger because I was scared—scared of losing you, too. Even after seeing Ballintino die and seeing pa dressed in his naval uniform morbidly stony… I can still feel them everywhere I go. It made me realize that we never truly die, do we? We are never really gone. I love you more than you can possibly imagine and if ever I go before you…just know that it wasn't your fault."*

I wiped the top of my hand across my nose before pulling away to leave. I posed hollow as if I were the living dead standing behind the bar. Susurri was seated beside Moira at a table near the jukebox. I stared so long and so hard that my eyes began to water.

Meanwhile, Kian was caught up speaking to some damn yuppie at the end of the bar. Irritated more than ever, I poured myself a shot of Jägermeister— gagging at the bitterness of licorice layered across my pallet.

Standing from her chair, Moira sauntered over to the bar taking the shot glass from my hand.

"Pour me one…" Watching my hardened expression, she became submissive. *"Please?"*

I tipped the bottle over filling it to the rim. Throwing it back without the bat of a lash, Moira licked the residue from her lips. *"Alius, dominus."* She smirked unchastely.

"What is it that you want, Moira?" My chest tightened.

"It isn't what I want, it's what you want." She slid the glass in my direction. *"Drink it."*

"I don't take orders from you or any other female around here."

Moira threw her head back with a cynical laugh. Leaning over the bar, she looped her arms around my neck. *"I know what you want...I watched you fuck her while you were inside me."*

"What a bold accusation..." My jaw clenched.

"I wouldn't dare pursue much further, Easton."

I gripped her wrists with warning, looking over her shoulder at Susurri. *"No one will believe you. So be careful of what you declare."*

A sensual gasp escaped into my ear as if my words meant nothing to her. *"I would find much pleasure in watching the outcome if you chose to inflict detriment and immoral erroneous upon you both."*

"And what is it you think it will bring? Benjamin is right, you are one mouthy bitch." I cut my eyes as a smile formed on her face.

"Mortem..." She whispered.

My eyes widened to its possible reality. *"Get the fuck away from me."* I shoved her out of my reach. *"You're an evil, pretentious woman and I bet it's because envy lurks in those veins."*

"You dare accuse me of false intent? How clever. How can I be envious over something I've already had? Hmm…if you're going to play the game, baby… you better learn to play dirty and up your level of expertise. 'Cause these guys won't give you another choice."

I shrugged off her insolence while pouring another shot. I wasn't going to allow anyone to get in the way of what I wanted. If the consequence of happiness brings you death in result, life isn't just a gamble, or a waiting game—it's fatal bullshit.

Standing outside with Adam only for the sole purpose to entertain him while he smoked a damn cancer stick, we watched shirtless members play a game of horseshoes. I noticed most members were covered in tattoos. Ones so old I could hardly give an accurate estimation on what they 'used to be'. The only one most shared that was specifically placed on their left pec looked like a Celtic styled anchor with the triquetra designed into the 'stock', forming both the eye and ring.

"Adam, do you bare the same marking as the rest?"

"I do. Funny how you are just now realizing we have a symbol."

"Well, you also had a wide range of opportunity to inform."

"Such a damn smartass." He chuckled. *"Well not much to tell, really. It is what it looks like. But the reason we created it was to resemble that we had found our home and freedom. The triquetra is a symbol just to show our strong belief of heritage and the power of three, like I had taught you about earlier on."*

"How do you earn the right to wear one?"

"Dedication, respect, and understanding true brotherhood through proper representation. Most of the elder members wear it on their left pec over their heart region. Here lately, Ryder and his sadistic minion, Benjamin, have decided to relocate the tattoo to be placed on the inner side of your left wrist. Those bastards are fucking changing all types of shit."

"So I've heard." I sighed.

"The reason we chose our chest was to keep class and keep it protected not due to shame or concealment. Just as a reminder that our breast is just as strong as the heart that beats beneath. Ryder wants people to know who we are and lives for the fear and entitlement. Things just aren't like they used to be. Yes, we were always a bunch of hardasses, what could you really expect? But, never like this. You have only scratched the surface of what these guys are about and what they are capable of. Drug trafficking, human trafficking, or sex slavery and pointless killings are what you assume and see in the

fucking movies. I'm not saying it hasn't happened in the past, our club just runs things differently."

Apparently, members have been caught using small game to transport drugs across state lines or use female members to conceal any type of paraphernalia. There have been times where members have ransacked homes for valuables just to pawn or exchange for other goods. Their ways to make money weren't as insane as I had thought—right then.

Tight quads and defined calves baring below ripped jean shorts strutted across my view, leaving my eyes to slowly raise to a fitted tank top suctioned to a tiny physique; prominently comforting a robust chest. Running finished nails through her bright hair, Susurri picked up a horseshoe, tossing it effortlessly.

The elegance of a delicate hand firmly gripped around iron sent eroticism throughout my body. The way her movement connected perfectly with the earth's gravitation left me breathless. Knowing she could feel my gaze each time my eyes fixated upon a beautiful rapture, killed me slowly when she'd rarely return the gesture.

Some members were arguing about some bullshit in the garage behind me, but I never paid them any mind. I just kept my remaining focus on my purpose as a rush of excruciating arousal burned at my nerve endings.

Susurri slowly raised her tank top above her naval, twisting the fibers between her fingertips while in wait. Sliding it up in haphazard above her head, she secured it through a belt loop; allowing everyone's eagerness to arise just to see underneath that black bikini top. *Damn.*

Dark boots kicked up dust to near her position as decorated fingers slid over her bare midriff to pull her into his chest. Pain struck me in the gut as I slightly began to hyperventilate. I couldn't take the torture; I couldn't bear seeing someone else touch her in the way I was meant to—in the way she wanted *me* to.

I ran inside finding seclusion within the cold walls of the beer cooler. I was infuriated, but I didn't have the right to be. What the fuck was my problem? It couldn't just be labeled infatuation or obsession. It wasn't passionate lust, either—I might have already loved her and damn her for not knowing it.

I grunted and groaned, throwing meaningless punches into the air to alleviate stress, but it only tired me. In the middle of my rant my eyes met a folded piece of paper tucked perfectly below the same rack Susurri clung to while in here with me. It was too neat to not have been meant for someone to see.

I bent down to pick it up and what unfolded was a little note…in fact what I have been longing for—a response. My eyes glanced over *'audeo tibi'* and I couldn't help but laugh to myself when my original statement was *'let me take you away'* translated in Latin.

I was still relatively new with the language so I didn't know everything. Sitting before my laptop alone in my bedroom, I researched its rendition. The bold print marked upon the screen was no other than the unpredicted. The words 'I dare you' stared back at me like an innocent victim.

****

The very next day, I found myself mangling underneath the hood of my father's Bronco, once again. Checking the oil level, I heard a loud rumble coming up from behind. Yanking the crowbar up from the ground, I quickly turned to see Adam without any other members...but had a passenger. Without any words, Susurri hopped off the backseat standing stuck in place.

Adam's eyes held emotional warning and I knew what he did would get us all killed. He never spoke; he just left her there standing before me with a timid and insecure posture.

"I got your note." I wiped an old tee shirt over my greased up chest.

Raising her sunglasses, her eyes remained fixated on my rugged contour. Slowly walking towards me, Susurri parted her lips barely inhaling. *"I know..."*

I drew my brows together attempting to take a step forward. Pressing the oiled fabric to dab the perspiration on my lips, she halted my movement.

"No, stop. Don't come any closer." Her chest heaved. *"...let me come to you."*

"Why?"

"Because, I have to remind myself that this was my choice to come here and see you."

Standing inches away, I flexed my chest feeling her soft hands make contact to its bareness. I stood motionless, allowing her to explore my body down to each rigid curve. Dragging the warmth of her lips across my tight flesh, her hot breath that barely braised its surface had my fists balled up. *"Do you want to know why Ryder keeps me so close?"* She breathed against me.

I tilted my head back to its pleasurable sensation. *"No. Why does he?"* I released a subtle groan.

"Because…" She smiled. *"I am untouched."*

My eyes shot open as I immediately looked down to grab her by the face. Staring deep into the eyes of inexperience with a dyer want to know, I instantly became hard. *"Why me?"*

"When you touch me, I get a feeling I have never felt before and I love it. It's like a rush better than any drug could ever give me. I want and crave it, I've even dreamt about it since the day you first laid hands upon me. You asked to take me away…but, I am here instead. Please let me know this is okay and that I didn't make a mistake."

Pulling her into me tightly, feeling the rattle of fear in her body tremble against me, I placed a solid kiss on her forehead. *"It wasn't a mistake."* I whispered. *"It was fate."*

Digging her nails into my back, I scooped her up onto my waist instantly crashing my mouth into hers. Sparks of contentment traveled through my face as my chest heaved tightly against hers. I wasted no time in getting her inside and into my bedroom. A moment I have waited dearly for had finally prevailed itself to me and I was going to relish in every second of it.

Laying her down gently atop the mattress, I hovered above her as she kissed my shoulder and down my arm. I wanted her to explore me at her own free will while I restrained my aggressive intensions.

"Easton, I want you to touch me in the way you have a thousand times in your mind."

Wetting my lips, I leaned down placing a trail of kisses down her neck while raising her shirt. Sitting up, Susurri pulled it off completely, leaving me to press my lips against her chest. Reaching my hand underneath her back, I unsnapped her bra feeling myself throb at the sight of perfect breasts. Dragging my grainy face across her soft flesh, I extracted my tongue running it over each mound as chills blanketed her body.

Making my way down her stomach, I slowly inched down her leggings. She clenched her thighs together with slight modesty and uncertainty. I wanted her to feel safe and to trust me as I sat back undoing my jeans.

The familiar sight of my member excited her as she bit her bottom lip, squirming beneath me. Wedging between her legs, I placed more kisses on the inside of her thighs witnessing glossy skin. Rubbing my facial hair over the softness, Susurri released a light sigh as my tongue glided in between her moist folds.

Needing to lubricate her more, I pulled her in by the ass, burying my tongue as far inside as I could while Susurri dug her nails into my scalp to grind against my mouth. Her taste was addicting, I didn't want to stop— but, I also wanted to feel her. I sought no pause as Susurri fell into unhesitant comfort as she fucked my face.

Pushing me away unable to handle anymore, I wedged myself between her legs softly gliding my erection against her swollen lips.

Susurri arched her back, clawing at my triceps. *"You are so hard."* She sucked in through her teeth. *"...is it going to hurt?"*

"Not for long, just hold onto me." I exhaled.

With a silent nod, she prepared herself for my entry as I placed my head against her opening, attempting to penetrate. Clenching her legs around me due to burning pain, Susurri took the risk of inviting me all the way in as I felt myself push through her hymen. A loud gasp escaped her mouth as she held onto me for dear life.

I thought of Adam and the story he told me about Renny; and just the same, I made love to Susurri as if she were my last. Considering it was her first time, Susurri couldn't make it much past the first thirty minutes, but swollen and sore, I felt Susurri crawl on top of me after a minor rest period we had dozed off during.

"I want more..." Her eyes were dangerously inviting.

I folded my hands behind my head with a prideful smile. *"Are you able to handle more?"*

Pressing her palms deep into my chest, I watched as she began gliding soft flesh against my growing erection. Bringing a hand to my face, I dropped my bottom jaw entering a thumb into my mouth. Eager to have her closer, I pulled her in with my other arm. Placing my wetted thumb pad against her tight pink flesh, I gazed harder at the sight of perfection, running my tongue along my lips as my mouth began to water.

"Why are you looking at me like that?" She whispered.

"Because, I have to have more..." I pulled her on top of my face assisting her with lubrication through oral pleasure.

The breath fell from her mouth as she planted both hands against the wall above my head. I never stopped nor slowed down until Susurri experienced her first orgasm, leaving her thighs to tremble and her back snapped into a human curved masonry. My hands gripped the softness of her ass to throw her over onto her back. I knew she wouldn't be able to handle being on top just yet, so I took the initiative to keep it missionary for the first day. I went until Susurri's claw marks threatened recently healed scars from my public display of punishment. I believed she had had enough by nightfall.

Lying against my chest, I could feel my heartbeat thud against her cheek while we made light conversation.

"You want to know something crazy?"

"What's that?" I asked inquisitively.

"Susurri is not my real name..." She went on. *"It's Cordelia, which means "jewel of the sea"."* She gave a subtle laugh.

"Why do they call you Susurri?"

"I was given the title when I was given bylaws to become a part of the club. They were to have been obeyed at all times and it was to never speak to another man unless given permission by Ryder. I told you I was untouched and he claimed me as a prized possession in a sense. I was kept a part from those types of men while growing up because things could have went in a terrible direction if anyone knew. Having a high position of power and authority, I felt safe being claimed by Ryder. No one ever questions his motives and never thinks twice to even curl their lip up. Now my name is all that I have...it's the only thing I know that truly belongs to me."

Guilt crept up my throat knowing I took a little piece of her, a part that was sacred while cradled by innocence. I will always carry that with me, even if that's all she gives me. *"Did you once believe Ryder would be the one to have you first?"*

"I did...before I met you. He is all I know, I always felt there was a part of me that was trapped. Having him constantly at my side knowing nothing could hurt me, I still felt somewhat imprisoned. With you, it gave me a sense of direction and curiosity I wanted to explore. At least I would finally know what it felt like— what I've been missing."

My head quickly jerked towards the window hearing a bike pulling up outside. I slid out from underneath Susurri to take a peek—it was Adam.

"Damn and he picks you up, too?" I chuckled.

Susurri reached down picking up her leggings to slide them on one leg at a time. Kneeling before her, I assisted with putting her boots back on. For a moment, she just stared at me before taking both hands to my face.

"What's wrong?" I overlapped them.

"I wish things weren't so difficult."

"As do I." I felt myself frown as she pressed a kiss to my forehead.

"If I could have met you sooner and go back…I'd only be yours. Forever."

I swallowed hard only returning my disappointment with a smile.

Sneaking into the kitchen, I held onto Susurri's hand guiding us through the darkness. Meeting Adam at the end of the yard, his eyes remained fixed on me.

"We all know what this little incident can cost, don't make me regret it, Easton. I swear I will come after you, myself."

I felt my Adam's apple drop heavily in my throat watching them pull away. For a moment, I stood still with my hands shoved deep into my pockets. It was one thing to piss Benjamin off, but to upset or disappoint Adam was another.

****

The following morning, my mother was seated at the kitchen table with a somber disposition. I figured I had a few moments to spare grabbing a cup of tea before heading out to the clubhouse. Pulling a chair out from across my mother, I slowly sat down as her eyes met mine.

"I am not going to highlight impertinent tackiness on your personal life, Easton. But please make sure you're using protection."

"Christ, ma. I am a grown man." I could feel my cheeks redden. *"I apologize if I awoke you with my nonsense, it's just…I know it doesn't matter to you. I have just been lonely."*

"Easton, just because I am a woman and just so happen to be your mother doesn't mean you can't talk to me about your feelings."

I pressed my lips together stopping myself from barking out another impulsive remark.

"I watched her leave last night. She looks cute. I would just be careful." My mother glanced down at her newspaper.

"Of what?"

"Those biker people you have recently involved yourself with. You've never even owned one, why the sudden interest?"

I became flustered with her sudden want to know about my daily activities. *"Ma…"*

"Look, I'm sorry. I would just like to know what is going on in my son's life considering you have been away for so long and you come home to only be away even more. I just don't understand. Is this some kind of rebellion? Are you afraid to be around me because of my condition?"

"Stop talking like that! No, it isn't rebellion…I just enjoy some of the people who find comfort in being a

*part of that life style. I didn't know there was anything
wrong with that."*

*"There isn't. At least let me meet the woman who
takes up my son's time every single day. I know you're
probably scared of losing me too, even if you don't want
to admit it. I can see it in your eyes—you have your
father's eyes for sure."* She smiled warmly.

"Thank you." I smiled. *"I am scared of something
going wrong."* I stood from my chair. *"I just have to do
this with my life, I feel I must."*

*"Why, has someone threatened you? Are you
okay?"*

*"Yes, yes I am fine. I can't explain it all. I really
don't want to so please don't make me. Just know that I
love you, okay?"*

"Easton, you're worrying me."

"Because, you're my mother." I pressed a strong
kiss to her forehead. *"Just trust me."*

It took every bit of strength I had to leave my
mother sitting there lonely and wondering. I wish I
didn't make it look so easy to walk off in the way I had
that day.

Thirteen

Adam took his seat at the table while Ryder began their meeting. I quietly stood by in observation when I could feel his glare flicker in my direction. Yet, it wasn't me who he had been watching as the clacking of wedges came across the floor leaving my eyes to follow Susurri strutting towards Ryder.

Jealousy burned my gut as she took a seat beside him, inviting the feeling of his hand placed upon her thigh. Gripping his hand in return, she took a glance my way; arching a peculiar brow. I did the same, trying to read her mind as if I could see the wheels turning within.

She never looked my way again until later on that evening. Kian and I were stuck behind the bar pouring shots and popping bottle caps for most of the evening so most members were beyond a legal limit. Sliding a glass down the bar, Moira was rested at the end. Motioning for me to pour another shot, I grabbed ahold of a Jameson bottle, filling it to the rim. Before I could give it back, I watched her move to the seat directly in front of me.

Laughing devilishly, I knew she was up to no good. *"Take the fucking shot, Easton."*

I gave an exhale through my nostrils, tossing it back. *"What are you up to now?"* I licked the residue from my lips.

"Always assuming I am inviting danger when I am only here to merely warn the dog who refuses to listen."

I leaned forward gritting my teeth. *"I don't know what the fuck you think you know, but I don't appreciate your constant attitude and willingness to piss me off."*

"I know a hell of a lot more than you think I do! And I don't need to hear it from Susurri's lips for proof."

She paused while deepening her stare. *"I bet her tight little cunt felt amazing around that large cock of yours. How did it feel taking that bitch's virginity?"*

I slammed my hands down, giving her wrists a tight squeeze. *"Watch your fucking mouth!"* I warned.

"I am wet at the sight of your masculine dominance." She scoffed. *"I can feel your anger serge through your grip. Looking in your eyes, I see your guilt…"* Moira smirked.

"You get pleasure from this don't you? You're fucking sick!" I hissed.

"No, I just hate to watch a good man fall so easily due to his stupidity and unrelenting egotism. You are just so far in the dark that you have no idea what you're getting yourself into."

"I am not falling for a damn thing." I bit out.

"Oh, but pretty baby…you most certainly are."

"What is it that you want? You want to feel me inside you? Are you jealous because you want me to yourself? Or that you don't want…" I stopped myself, watching her mouth open with excitement waiting to hear the truth spill from my lips.

"That I don't want what? Listen here, Easton. I can have you if I really wanted to. I already have…and it's amazing watching the things you do once pushed too far. God, it's amazing witnessing weakness…everyone

has it. Don't pride yourself on believing you are capable of masquerade against the most well-known human flaws." Leaning closer to my ear, Moira pierced my ear with a venomous principle. "*You love someone you can and never will have.*"

I felt my heart drop into my stomach as she turned to leave. Moira seemed conniving and finicky from the get go, now she was beginning to freak me out with her riddled tongue. I looked across the room to see Susurri rested in Ryder's lap while he had a beer with Benjamin and Chad.

Adam waltzed up noticing my peeved posture. I nearly shoved my fist through the bottom of a glass stein watching Moira fall all over Benjamin like the damn slut she was.

"*You had better be careful of that woman. She's wicked and if you let her sink her fangs in, she will pull you down with her.*"

"*I ain't too worried about her. She's just a bitch who fucks shit up when she throws a tantrum after not getting her way.*" I replied smugly.

"*You messed around with her, didn't you?*"

My eyes glared as I continued wiping the inside of the glass over and over to control my urge to throw it across the room. Even if Susurri had entrusted Moira with whatever secrets she loved to spill, it still gave Moira no right to badger me with her bullshit.

Shaking his head with disappointment, Adam gave a sigh. *"Damnit kid, are you ever going to learn?"*

"I thought she didn't belong to anyone?"

"Ha…not just anyone…she belongs to Benjamin. He was her first and always will remain so."

"So why is it he hasn't beaten my ass for even touching her?"

"Because he knows that anything goes and if he tells her to do something, she knows she ought to or punishment will follow."

"That's just fucking ridiculous! So not only did I fuck Benjamin's little bitch, but I have also…"

Adam slammed his hand over my mouth before I could finish. *"You better hush it now, boy."* His eyes enlarged. *"I don't want to hear about it or talk about whatever "didn't" happen. You got it?"*

Remembering the fact of him beating my ass if any of us were to be caught cycled a loop in my mind. I pulled his hand from my mouth hearing the scratch of my facial hair drag across his palm. Handing him a bottle of beer, we made a silent agreement to discontinue as he walked off.

The duration of the night I got to endure the rush of fire coursing through my veins each time I caught a glimpse of Ryder pressing his lips against Susurri's neck, each moment his hands ran down her torso, each grip to her ass and thighs as the hairs on my neck stood up with rage. Making random eye contact with me throughout the night had me all the more pissed off as if she was enjoying the torment she was putting me through. If I could, I would have jumped over this damn bar and slammed her down onto the pool table for causing me such agony.

Instead, I waited until Susurri followed Ryder and a few others out for a smoke break. I crept my way to the side of the clubhouse, keeping my huntsman gaze upon her every move. As dangerous as this was, I had no control of what my mind longed for—my body longed for.

Watching them begin to walk inside, I sprinted as quietly as possible up behind her, grabbing her by the arm. Before she could gasp with fear, I covered her mouth pulling her around to the back of the building. The moon cast a perfect shadow across her glistening eyes as they flickered with curiosity.

"How dare you tease me like that?" I exasperated, crashing my mouth into hers.

I pushed her up against the wall interlocking our hands above her head as we struggled to breath. Pressing my ossifying pelvis against her, I shot my hands to the front of her shorts undoing them in frenzy.

"Easton, we can't do this here!" She panted.

"Next time you should reconsider your actions." I continued to undo my jeans.

Dropping her shorts, I hoisted her up onto my waist pushing my way inside to feel her maturing self-lubrication.

"Oh, my God…" The breath left her as she grimaced in slight pain.

Pushing my way into moist tissue, I felt her tightness suction around my member as her body reacted to intercourse leaving warm liquid layered my skin. *"That's it…stay wet just like that."* I groaned, slowly sliding in and out completely enjoying myself.

As her skin stretched around me I felt my lower abdomen meet hers as I entered fully for the first time. The shock had her jaw drop as her muscles tightened throughout her body. Intensifying her clutch around my neck, I penetrated once more with a bit more force as she fought to inhale. I could tell it began to feel good once Susurri absentmindedly assisted in friction by grinding into me as I picked up speed. Unable to remain slow, I slammed into her until she was numb. Clamping her teeth into my neck, Susurri gave a hard suck while attempting to control her noise. It only caused me to drive even deeper as her vocals stilled until convulsing into a hard orgasm. Gripping her thighs even more, I kept going to reach my release. Lasting only three more eager strokes, I pulled out pumping my release onto her inner thigh.

Placing Susurri back to the ground, I heard a rustle in the trees to my right as I lowered my breathing. Panic set in as I looked through blackness trying to pinpoint a figure, but nothing revealed itself. I looked down into Susurri's eyes as she fastened her jean shorts.

"You're a very bold man."

"I just go after the things I want most and that just so happens to be you."

"Just remember where we are, Easton. You have a place just as I do." She began adjusting her hair.

I grabbed her by the face, looking deep into her eyes. *"My only place is anywhere with you."* I gave her a gentle kiss as she overlapped my hands with hers.

Things could have taken a deadly turn for the both of us, but I didn't care. My heart screamed louder than a bullet leaving a barrel. I wasn't sure if I would see daylight most times lately, I wasn't even sure who the hell I was turning into. I knew one thing was for certain and it was that nothing compared to the indescribable way she made me feel each time she was around.

With no words spoken, Susurri ran a hand down my scruffy cheek with a side smirk—as if she had worry in her mind, maybe even a fear of some sort. I grabbed her hand before she became out of reach.

"Don't stop yourself from loving me back…"

A mild smile pulled up her cheeks as she gave my hand a reassuring squeeze. *"How selfish would I be if I were to?"*

Benjamin's gaze shot through me as I reentered the clubhouse making my way to the cooler. Kian had asked me to replace the Miller keg twice and I still managed to forget. Feeling chill bumps dance across the surface of my arms as I reached down to pick up the unexpected weight, I heard the door fly open. Taking a shove to my back, I tipped forward dropping the keg onto my foot.

"God fucking damnit!" I turned to see Benjamin behind me.

"I don't even know what to say to you right now…"

"What the fuck are you talking about?"

Benjamin curled his fingers into a fist with a crack sending it straight into my mouth. *"You know exactly what the fuck I am talking about. Matter of fact, come on…we're going for a fucking ride, now!"* He shouted.

I let go of the keg, exiting the cooler as he followed rather closely. My tongue continuously ran over my busted lip as metallic waved across my pallet.

"Kian, get the fuck over here dampnas!" Benjamin barked. *"Ryder, we need to take these two for a ride."*

Ryder immediately hopped up from his seat. *"Quid hoc malorum est?"*

"I'll explain when we get there."

Shoving us both outside beneath the street light, fear rose in my stomach for the first time since I've been here.

"Get the fuck on your bikes and let's go!" Ryder commanded.

We followed their lead through miles and miles of woods until reaching the luminous liveliness of the city. We stopped in front of a local bar, parking out front. I was familiar with the area, but never hung around after hours.

"Mouere ualet!" Benjamin gave me a shove.

Making our way down a darkened alleyway, I could see the silhouette of someone rested against the brick wall.

"Let me ask you something, Easton. How much dedication do you have to us?"

I twitched my nostril with defiance. *"He asked you a fucking question."* Ryder snarled.

"Enough..."

"Enough for what, exactly? Enough to save someone's life? You see, Easton...in order to find where someone's heart is, you typically place them in a situation

in order to find it." Benjamin smirked while whipping out his pocket knife. *"Not everyone has someone to care for them. Some people, no one gives a fuck about. In our club we offer protection and brotherhood unlike any other. This fella next to me I'd die for and I'd kill for…would you die for those standing around you? Would you kill for us?"* His eyes narrowed. *"The man crouched down is an innocent vagabond, no one misses him… no one cares where the fuck he is. Therefore, no one will miss him and no one will come looking for him."*

"What are you getting at?" I felt my heart rate rise.

Taking a ferocious step forward, Benjamin struck his hand to my holster placing his face flush with mine. *"If Ryder could only see what I do…"* He whispered.

Jerking my gun from its holster, Benjamin cocked the slide back aiming it at Kian. He stood pale with a trimmer. *"You either shoot the man, or I blow the kid's fucking head off."*

I couldn't believe Benjamin was serious, I thought for sure he had lost his mind much less his temper. Due to my hesitant reaction, Benjamin stepped forward placing the gun to my forehead. *"This is the second time I have held your own weapon against you. I could only imagine how pathetic of a Marine you must've been. Jesus fuck. Take the fucking gun, nequam!"* He moved his aim back over towards Kian.

"All right." I put my hands up.

With a sardonic laugh, Benjamin slammed the gun into my chest. I neared the old man cautiously as the pistol vibrated in my grip. I could feel my face become flushed as I fought to keep my tears at bay. I could hear Kian's shallow breathing as he crept up behind me.

"Come on, nequam. Show me just how loyal and dedicated you are...show me how far you are willing to go for those you care so deeply for."

He said it as if he knew something I didn't. As if he knew exactly how I felt towards Susurri, but I doubted it. Forcing me to take an innocent man's life was against everything I stood for, or was it?

"It could be no worse than you killing the innocence in their own home. How courageous and honorable of you to take something that doesn't belong to you." His tone became threatening.

I raised the pistol as the man released a raspy cough. I couldn't do it; I could feel tears running down my face as my heart pounded in my chest. *"Please...don't make me do this."* I begged.

"You will fucking do it or I will end your fucking life!" Benjamin's voice echoed.

Running up behind Kian, I turned to see Ryder snatch his head back placing a knife to his throat. The tears echoing in his breathing had me cry even harder.

"I guess he doesn't value us, Ryder. How about that? He can kill one of us...but he can't kill a waste lying to rot."

"I will not fucking die over your ignorance or withdraw of glorious integrity." Kian escaped from Ryder's grip taking both hands to my pistol.

Within milliseconds, Kian pressed my index into the trigger, firing a shot that had the man instantly slump over. In that exact moment I couldn't breathe, I couldn't think, I couldn't register reality as I stood crazed over what just happened. In slow motion, I watched them look at one another before turning to leave the scene—without worry or fear. I didn't waste any time in running after as I slammed my pistol back into its holster.

Before pulling out, Benjamin looked back at me over his shoulder with a blank stare. I had to fight from further emotion on the ride back to the clubhouse before I blurred my vision to the point of crashing. I knew killing that man would never set right with me, but it was as if it were my test for an initiation.

Once we got back to the clubhouse, Ryder and Benjamin hauled us inside yelling with overjoy. Grabbing bottles from behind the bar, I was slammed onto the pool table as alcohol was forced into my mouth. Benjamin asked a fellow member to get his tattoo gun and engrave the club's symbol on my chest in its original location—the left pec.

I winched through the pain, watching myself bleed as more and more alcohol entered my system. I hardly remembered anything else from then on since I blacked the fuck out.

The next moment I voluntarily opened my eyes, I was lying face down into my pillow. I had a hard time sitting up, feeling a burning sensation on my chest. My shirt was stained with blood as it stuck to my new branding. It was the same tattoo every member earned once patched. I didn't quite understand why they didn't just place it on my wrist like most of the newer members had. And if pointless killing was their way of initiation, then I truly had no idea on what the fuck mayhem I had gotten myself into.

I took a deep breath pulling the crusted fabric from my skin, hearing it tear away. Unbuttoning my shirt to look at my wound, it was covered in a dry layer of blood. It was tender beneath my fingertips as I glided rough pads over the area. Reddened flakes fell below as I uncovered the club's symbol marked upon my chest.

Was I now one of them? Is this what it takes to be the baddest kid out there so everyone fears you? Is this what everyone had to do just to prove themselves and their dedication? I bared no honor, no respect and no soul. I was just as ruthless and diseased as they were. Or did it mean something else? Was this proof that I had lost my mind…after everything I have been through and have witnessed—this was my outcome? To be branded with the mark of a dead man…a man who lost his way and can only find one road to walk. Lurk down the valley in the shadow of death, bringing detriment and carnage to those around him. Will I ever

be the same? Will I ever find forgiveness... or will forgiveness forsake me?

Fourteen

*F*or days, I couldn't look myself in the mirror; much less look my mother in the eyes while she spoke to me. I haven't had a good night's rest in over a week as I walked around in a zombified silence, dragging my boots across the dirt just like I had through reddened sand more times than I liked to keep count of. The itch on my chest was a constant reminder of my heinous insanity with a never-ending memory. I didn't allow the incident to break me; if anything, I let it change me.

Each day I wake, I haven't felt the same—I haven't felt like myself. If I had the power to reverse time, I'd change every mistake I had ever made. I'd much rather had been pegged with a shard of metal through the skull to save me from surviving this living hell that has taken me over.

Ballintino used to always say 'it's funny how the greatest of tragedies happen to those less fortunate and the most fortunate opportunities life has to offer are granted by luck, or to those undeserving.' I never appreciated the value of his wisdom; I just laughed it off, telling him he was full of shit. Now that my world took a jerk to its gravitational pull...I have been thrown into a clusterfuck disaster where the only one I felt I could trust was me. I hanker to prove my self-value...my self-worth, but not for it to amount to pride so weak it dissolves within a subtle smile of acceptance.

As distant as I have become, most nights I could care less to see daylight. But even death wouldn't keep them from coming after me. I think about what my mother would do without me—or if she knew about any of this at all? She may have spotted Susurri's exit, but she hasn't seen the things that I've done lately.

The last person I'd ever want to disappoint would have been my father. Would he forgive me and find in his heart an understanding as to why I have been forced to do the things I had? Would he save me? Or would he let me fall due to my own mistakes?

I feel I have done all I can, I have watched ones

closest to me wither away and take their last breath. It was almost beyond a state of acceptance—it was all I knew. I claim to know so little about love, but what I knew wasn't real. The desire my eyes held to draw in her sight, the ache my body condensed down to the core of my bones until they almost shattered and the burning in my gut each time my fingers brush against her soft flesh; that to me is what love should feel like.

I stood before my bathroom mirror gazing into darkened eyes from the lack of sleep. I pressed the tips of my forefingers against my cheeks, digging them into my overgrown stubble. I chose to leave it with just a few trims to tidy it up. I wear the mark of the beast and I sure as hell fit the mold with the way I've been looking lately; despite my recent actions.

Down at the clubhouse, Adam was the first to approach me as I entered.

"Hey, I grabbed you a few things while I was out. They made me think of you." He held out an 'Afghanistan War Veteran' patch and another that read 'Improvise, Adapt, Overcome' with the eagle, globe and anchor on the right-hand side.

I felt myself smile while receiving them in my hand. *"Thank you."*

"The best person I know who could sew those on for you is Renny."

I raised my brows meeting his sympathetic eyes. *"You know I can't talk to her, Easton. Just go over and ask her. She's sweeter than Tennessee's honey."*

I shrugged, making my way over where she was seated. Of course Moira and Susurri were hanging about, making small talk about whatever the hell it was women found so damn interesting.

"Easton." Moira laced her fingers below her chin.

"Moira…" I glared. *"I wanted to ask you a favor, Renny."*

"Watch out Renny, this one here is dangerous." She scoffed.

Susurri rested her face against her palm, ignoring Moira's nonsense.

"Sic, ubi prospectu?" Her eyes remained easy.

"She speaks but broken English. If need be, I'll translate." Susurri offered.

My lips parted as I watched her communicate with Renny. *"Just ask her if she wouldn't mind sewing on some patches for me, please?"*

Susurri translated as Renny softly smiled with a nod.

"Ut et confunde eos, sed potens est in gullas." Moira belted out with laughter.

The blush upon Renny's cheeks was not in the same fashion as the agape embarrassment flushed across Susurri's face. I swallowed hard trying to figure out why Moira would have just said that in front of Susurri.

"Te fututam eum?" Susurri asked in bewilderment.

"Non, futui me..."

The dropping of Susurri's mouth had heat radiating from my chest, knowing what their argument was over. Benjamin and Ryder came rushing over the second Susurri jumped across the table to beat Moira's ass. Caterwauling all over the hardwood, Benjamin yanked them apart while Ryder stood disappointed with Susurri's impulsive lashing out.

"Quid futuo?" He yelled. *"Why are we arguing, ladies?"*

"She's a fucking slut...that's why." Susurri muttered under her breath.

Ryder snatched Moira by her bottom jaw, forcing her to look him in the eyes. *"Whatever little debacle of estrogen that just occurred had better find its resting place. Understood?"*

"Yes, dominus fortis..." Her eyes darted towards Susurri's, then mine.

"Susurri...officium, nunc!" He barked.

With a roll of her eyes, Susurri stormed off with a huff as Ryder quickened his steps right behind. While stuck in place watching their exit, I could hear Benjamin and Moira having a light argument almost in a whisper. Their Latin was too fast for me to comprehend everything. All I picked up was Benjamin explaining that 'he knows' over and over, trying to calm her down.

I watched Moira try to wave him off until he grabbed her by the wrists. *"Don't make me do this out here."* He gritted his teeth.

Meeting my eyes over his shoulder, Moira leaned in giving Benjamin a tender kiss. *"Me Paenitet."*

Benjamin pressed his lips against hers once again before excusing her. *"Don't think your time isn't coming, nequam."* He glared.

Shoving his hand against my chest to walk through me, Benjamin moved by. Renny's eyes were still on mine as she side smirked, holding out her hands.

"You sure?"

She motioned for me to take off my cut with a nod. I gently laid it in her hands with a thank you. Turning to leave, I felt Renny tighten her grip around my wrist. *"He only warns when something bad is to come."* Her thick accent caused my tongue to tingle.

I had nothing to say, I just closed my mouth and turned to leave. Adam waved me over towards the bar, inviting me into his and Kian's conversation.

"Easton, do you mind going to grab a bottle of Fireball from the cooler?"

Knowing I had a reason to eavesdrop on Ryder and Susurri, I got right to it. Instead of taking a right towards the cooler, I tiptoed to the left to peer inside Ryder's office. With her back against the wall, I could see Susurri standing in fear as Ryder pressed his hands into her thighs. Keeping their foreheads together, Ryder lowered his tone.

"What has she done that has angered you so much?" He demanded to know.

"I just despise the way she whores herself around is all."

"Fuck what the bitch does. It shouldn't matter to you for any reason other than..." He paused before taking a step back. *"Susurri... what in the fuck have you done?"* His hand landed across her face.

Interrupting my opportunity to listen further, I felt my shirt being yanked down the hallway. Adam dragged me down to the cooler before my inner rage had the chance to act on impulse. Once we were safe inside, his reddened face and wide eyes beamed in the lightening. *"Let me see your chest..."*

"What?"

"Let me see your goddamn chest!" He marched over to me ripping my buttons open. Seeing my tattoo, he roughly ran his hands across, forcing me to wince from irritating scabbed over skin. Placing his hand to his goatee before giving it a disgruntled stroke, Adam shook his head. *"They've made a mockery out of you…"*

"What the fuck do you mean?"

"Remember how I told you they changed its location? Well, it's because no one nowadays wears it on their chest. That regards the club's olden days…like the old testament if you will."

"Why did they carve something so outdated into my chest?"

"Because, you must have disrespected them to the point they are going to make an example out of you. To put you in a position of shame to disrespect you right back. Christ, Easton… I don't know what the fuck you've done, but what's to come isn't good—for you."

"But you know?"

Adam ran at me placing his hand over my mouth. *"I know nothing of what you've done. I only have assumed! I only did what was asked of me. I should have known they were up to something greater."* His voice trailed off.

"What you were asked? Wait…what the fuck do you mean by that? Were you asked to bring her to me?"

Adam shook me off saying no over and over again.

"Goddamn it, Adam! Tell me what the fuck is going on!" I grabbed his arm.

His expression turned to stone as he looked down at my hand. *"Remember your fucking place, Easton!"* He jerked away. *"Grab the damn Fireball and get the fuck out."*

Yanking the bottle from the shelf, I gripped the glass within my frustration. *"You lend great wisdom, you offer to help me and you teach me about brotherhood…"*

"You know nothing about brotherhood!" He intervened. *"This isn't the fucking Marine Corps, Easton. This is our life! I told you that if you couldn't play nice and learn to follow the rules that severe consequences were sure to follow. You can thank God for making your stubbornness prominent and foolish decisions come often."*

"No, I know all there is to know about brotherhood." I stood inches away from his face, trying to control emotions that itched behind my eyes. *"I know what it's like to watch a brother die before me."*

"Good, now we all share the same feeling…the same loss of someone who meant more than the sky and stars above. Your "brothers" differ from mine…yours were not dangerous. They placed themselves in danger. You better figure out your strength real quick like and

prepare for whatever comes your way. This isn't a goddamn friendly meet at Harley on a Sunday morning." In a flash, he exited the cooler.

Smashing the bottle against the wall, I screamed—screamed so loud my vocals gave out as I gasped for air. What do I have to do to get the fuck out of this alive? I was damned if I let these fuckers kill me…I am a Devil Dog, I do not bow to the enemy. I do not negotiate with the foreign and I never disrespect my founding fathers.

"I must shoot straighter than the enemy who is trying to kill me…what counts in war is not the rounds we fire, the noise of our burst, or the smoke we make. It's the hits that count. We will hit." I repeated to myself.

I know my purpose and I know my place; if it was going to be here then I had to be better at the game they played. I must remain two steps ahead and never allow them access to my vulnerability or passage to manipulate my mind. I am the best of the best, I am fierce, I am mighty, I am the strongest…and I *will* survive.

I slid my way through the boodle of drunken fucks crowding the clubhouse, bringing my embittered angst to stand behind the bar as I remained brooding for the majority of the night. I knew I had gotten under Adam's skin, but I gained a different mindset within the last sixty seconds of my life as I had a relapse of anger wash over me. Drowning in the want to run…to get away as anxiety pinched my throat, preventing a proper breath to enter my lungs.

My chest heaved as I puffed my cheeks watching Benjamin's derisive gaze hold me under weigh as if he could see me gasping for air. I have never allowed others to conquer my emotions until I involuntarily became involved with these people.

Catching a near missed glance of Susurri's backside walking outside, I dropped my hand towel on the bar top to follow. *"Hey, Kian... keep watch. I'll return shortly."*

Leaned up against the wall towards the end of the clubhouse, Susurri dropped her face into her palms as she tried keeping her sobs to minimal of sound. Without even second guessing who was lurking about, my feet carried me quickly in her direction; pulling her away from the wall and around the corner out of sight.

"What did he say to you?" I cupped her jaw. *"Look at you...you're upset! Did he hurt you?"*

"Easton, stop! It doesn't concern your worry."

"The fucking hell it doesn't! I saw the way he touched you...I watched the fear rise in your eyes. You should never cry...not over a wrongful touch or misdirected anger." I took the pads of my thumbs to her falling tears. *"Look me in the eyes...please?"*

She sighed with frustration. *"What do you want from this, Easton?"* I could see the anger burning in her eyes.

"I want you to fucking run away with me! Get away from here for good!" I panted.

A subtle laugh of disbelief escaped her quivering lips. *"Yeah…sounds like a dream come true. But, what you don't understand is that if we go…they will stay after us until we are found and they will kill us! Is that what you want? Eminent death?"* She searched my eyes.

"Of course not! I just don't want to be a part of this… you shouldn't be a part of this!" I growled.

"You chose your path as I chose mine…willingly or not, this is still my home. These people are my family. Would you just up and leave yours if you had nowhere else to go? What would your mother think?"

Her words hit me like a bullet straight to the gut. I understood the want for family—for love. But, I knew this wasn't the right way. Not for her and certainly not for me.

"Susurri…" Her gaze sharpened to my tone. *"I want you with me. Do you not understand how badly I want to be with you? I can protect you…"*

"No, you can't! There are Disciple chapters all over this goddamn country…there are only so many places we can possibly hide. I don't want to spend my life running…" Her eyes veered off. *"… and neither should you."*

"I will run until my heart implodes in my fucking chest if I know I have you by my side through the entirety.

Would you have become so territorial against Moira if you didn't feel the same?"

Her eyes reacquainted mine, drowning in mistrust. *"Easton…"*

"Shh…just stop and think for a minute." I took her in by the face.

Pressing her soft lips against mine streaming a hot rush through my body, I could feel her grip tighten on my arms as if she didn't want to let me go. Time didn't exist, the world's motion slowed just to allow me the fragment of an enjoyable forbidden moment.

"Its impossibility is greater than you know." She pulled away with a whisper.

Taking my hands from her face, Susurri dropped them while leaving me to stand alone in the darkness. Balling my fist, I slammed it against the wall as pain shot up to my elbow. *"Nothing is impossible…we are just so consumed by laziness and skeptical hesitance that we fear what is to come if we were to actually try."* I bit out.

Fifteen

Benjamin was going over the event schedule for our annual toy run. It was one of the largest charities the Disciples took part in for the sole purpose of kosher social publicity and belief in helping our own. It was hard to believe that any of these guys cared about anyone other than their damn selves.

Besides the Toys for Tots run, they also took part in the Wounded Warrior ride for our armed forces Veterans. I could personally appreciate the reason for the gathering of our nation's very own heroes. Adam claimed 'we take care of our own before anything. Americans will always be true family.' Despite riding for a meaningful purpose, most members just used it as a social excuse to drink and have a good time.

Susurri had chosen to once again place us on a verbal suspension these past few days and the worst part about it was, I fucking hated every second.

Dark stilettos glided across the lot, kicking up dust that led a trail straight to Ryder's bike. Throwing a practiced leg over to rest upon the granted throne, Susurri made herself comfortable against the sissybar.

The sight of her arms wrapping around Ryder's abdomen threw my expression into disgruntlement. Feeling heat radiate through the thick leather comforting my torso, a hand slid down my left shoulder. Looking into my rearview, I could see Moira masked behind her shades with silk chocolate strands pulled back neatly with the clubs bandana. Tight, holey, and tattered cut off jean shorts clung to olive thighs beneath the 'Rosie the Riveter' persona she had going on.

I felt an eyebrow arch as I mentally appreciated Moira's company for the first time ever. She wasn't all too horrible; she was just a primitive bitch who knew what was expected of her. Meanwhile, being tortured with minimal freedom—she found great pleasure in stretching her limitations.

Sliding her arms around my stomach, Moira leaned in towards my ear. *"Hope you don't mind a passenger. You've been looking rather lonely, here lately."*

I gave a shrug focusing on Ryder's signal for us to start our engines. We had six rough hours to Indiana ahead of us. Ryder chose to leave later in the day that way we could camp out the night before the event. I think he just wanted to get away for a while and I didn't argue with the brief escape plan.

Kian was positioned alongside of me in the beginning, but ended up drifting to the back halfway through our trip. I became relaxed as Moira absentmindedly began tickling my ribs by running her nails up and down the fabric of my shirt. My breathing deepened the more her touch intensified. Only after realizing my enjoyment did Moira then reach underneath to dig into my flesh.

A rugged breath burst into the harsh wind attacking my face as Moira's chest pressed firmly against my back. Nails soon traveled from my abdomen leading down to my beltline. She began to undo my jeans but I struck my left hand to pause her movement. With disagreement, Moira jerked my hand away to shove hers down inside.

Flaccid for but a moment, I felt myself harden as her grip tightened around me. Slowly stroking until I completely solidified, Moira didn't falter to an exhausted forearm until I glazed the surface of the gas tank.

We stopped for fuel about an hour outside the state line and I jumped off the bike to quickly clean up the mess stained across Adam's paint job. Dropping the pump down inside the tank, Moira came waltzing up offering me an energy drink.

I smiled with gratitude popping the tab. *"Thank you."*

"I can take care of you, Easton. You just have to let me." She placed a bottle of water to her lips.

Chugging the can, I crushed the aluminum within my palm before slamming it into the trash receptacle. *"I don't need to be taken care of."*

"Your member says otherwise…" Her voice lowered.

Gritting my teeth, I gave the pump one last squeeze before jerking it out to hang it back. *"There is more to me than what pleases my "member"."*

"A heart that beats…" She placed a hand to my chest. *"You lock it up…yet it dares to explode with tangible emotion you hold captive. Too bad you long to love someone who will never…love you back."*

"Why are you so concerned with how I feel towards her?" I bit out.

Moira smiled at my verbal admittance. *"Because, I can see how smart of a man you truly are, but you are acting stupid! I do not want to see what could possibly happen if there were to ever come a day the damn devil himself shines light upon your misdeeds, Easton. I shall feel no remorse and none of them."* Her eyes scanned the members around us. *"Will shed mercy for you and whoever else is involved."*

"You are involved in a way, now aren't you?" I stepped forward, gazing into her eyes. *"I'm sure things would be terrible for us all."*

"Don't threaten me with false accusations. It's Susurri that you're placing in grave danger. Would you forgive yourself if you placed her in harm's way? Could you live with the fact of what you will cause?"

A devilish smile pulled my cheeks back. *"A snake crawls on his belly to remain unnoticed for he was damned to do so. His skin matches the earth for the purpose of adaptation and camouflage. He poses dangerous only when one becomes intrusive in his domain. If provoked, he strikes to protect his life and what is his…"*

"Though the quickness of his tongue runs deeper than the venom he threatens to pierce through the flesh of his enemy. When you cross a predator much larger in scale, your bite would be but a bee sting to these rabid titans you dare challenge. Choose your approach wisely, Easton. Why start a war you are damned to lose? After all…these gentlemen are your makers." A brow twitched above her smile.

"Because, sometimes the war we place ourselves in wasn't by fucking choice!"

"Says the Marine of valor?" Moira scoffed.

Leaving me to continue the last part of the ride to be alone, I straddled the bike watching her hop on the back of Benjamin's. Kian's expression seemed concerned for my sake as he shook his head.

I enjoyed the last hour in pleasurable solitude watching the sun dip down in the western sky. We pulled up to what looked like a huge campground with tents scattered about the premises like some biker Woodstock ordeal. Most clubs hung with their own members and then you had those who wanted to mingle with everyone.

Kian and I hung out with Adam for the majority of the night until my memory became a blur after the intake of at least ten beers. Having shown up with over fifteen riders strong, most of us had to pitch our own tent or crash in the grass on a blanket somewhere.

Rested in a lawn chair by a huge campfire, I loosely held a half emptied bottle of Coors in my right hand. Looking through the flames, I could see Moira making her way over in my direction. Though, to my surprise she targeted Kian, instead of me—thank God.

Leaning into his ear, she began whispering some drunken slurs that seemed to be humorous in Kian's opinion. Without a word, she took him by the hand wandering off into the darkness.

My eyes remained half open as I struggled to bring in the clarity of my surroundings. I put the bottle to my lips, inhaling the last of its contents before tossing it into the fire.

Slump in my chair, I could feel myself beginning to doze off. Before I knew it, I was lying flat on my back inside of someone's tent. The first time I actually opened my eyes to realize where I was, I remember looking up into the ceiling of the tent. Blinking several times, the alcohol I consumed hours ago had overpowered my want to sit up or fully awaken. To suppress nausea, I fell back into a deep slumber feeling my head spin.

Breathing in slowly, the sound of a zipper had me twitch to consciousness. My eyes shot forward to the door flap opening with a tiny hand spreading the entryway. Poking her head through, I watched Susurri climb in fearlessly and determined. Too numb to move, I mumbled a greeting with struggle as she zipped the door shut.

Turning on all four to face my direction, I watched Susurri crawl on top of me in a prowling manner. I moved my hands to take ahold of those wanting hips as she slowly grinded into me. I was still slightly dizzy as I relaxed beneath her weight. Grabbing my hands, Susurri interlocked our fingers while placing my arms above my head.

"Keep them there." She demanded.

Cold fingertips dove beneath my shirt landing against the skin of my ribcage, slowly making their way to my pecs. Flexed and heaving beneath her touch,

Susurri dropped her bottom jaw with a sigh to my solidified contour.

She removed her hands, tugging at the end of my shirt. *"Take this off."*

I raised my arms to assist her while she stripped the fabric covering my hardened torso. Taking both hands to her tank top, I watched it peel up and over her head as she was quick to unsnap her bra. The sight of perfectly round breasts had my throat closing in with the inability to swallow.

An unsteady breath had my lips twitching as Susurri advanced to undo her shorts. Erotic intensity pulled at my gut like an imbedded blade seeing her excitement rise the moment of revealing black string. My eyes followed the thin strand that rode alongside the definition of her hip. Without hesitation, Susurri inched them down just enough for me to view her entire front side hidden by silk fibers.

Eagerness magnetized my grip to the waist of her shorts with a deadly jerk. Pulling her down into the rigidness that throbbed between her legs, Susurri planted her palms into my chest releasing a desirable moan.

"Take them off…" I whispered.

Elevating upward into a stance, Susurri shoved her shorts to the floor and left the scraps of seduction for a tease. Lowering herself back onto my waist, she inched downward onto my thighs to undo my jeans. Freeing my aching erection from suffocation, Susurri placed me between her legs, gliding the silk fibers against my skin. I could feel the fabric dampen the more she moved up and down, arousing herself.

Unable to withstand much more, I took out my pocket knife—flicking the blade open. A sparkle of curiosity lit her eyes on fire as I slid it underneath the string on her hip, upturning the razor edge to slice straight through. The breath fell from her mouth as I did the same to the opposing side.

Taking the knife from my hand, Susurri placed it to her tongue with a seductive gesture. Lowering my gaze, I could see barren flesh with swollen lips longing to engulf my every inch. She has never been on top— but I wasn't going to stop her, either. Her devouring eyes overpowered any possible doubt in her mind.

Rising up to place my tip at her entrance, natural lubrication trickled down my skin as I slowly penetrated through tightened tissue. The further I entered the more shallow my breathing had become. Susurri gritted her teeth with a wince as I lifted my hips to enter fully; keeping a steady grip on her hips.

Taking a moment to adjust, Susurri placed a hand to her lower abdomen and the other to my chest. I knew she could feel how deeply embedded I was and even though it produced subtle pain, Susurri picked up her speed increasing her vocals each time I reentered her. We were going much faster than I ever anticipated from her so early. But she was in a wanting mood and I was willing to give her whatever she needed.

I placed my hands on the smooth of each breast,

gently messaging them in my palms as Susurri rode me to her satisfaction. Outlining her entire physique with a laser stare, my hands traced up and down each curve; nearly losing the oxygen in my lungs. I wanted more—I had to have more…so without warning, I sat up lifting myself from the ground while holding her stiffly into me. I shoved myself in as deep as I could go, hearing an aggressive moan leave the depths of Susurri's throat as she pulled my face into her chest.

Her nails sent a fiery sensation like Gazelles blazing a field as they dug into my scalp. I kept driving deeper until I felt her thighs trembling against my ribcage as the peak of my orgasm had me release uncontrollably inside of her. Both hands flew to my face as she drew me in for a hard kiss. A force so strong, I refused to pull away as a tsunami rush of my mind's predilection promised eruption.

Falling to my back, Susurri fell too; panting against my chest while trying to slow her breathing and control the spasms of her muscles. A small moment of silence ensued with only echoes of exhalation vaporizing through the air.

"Why won't you leave with me?"

Susurri rubbed a hand up and down my forearm. *"I'm scared…"*

"Scared of what? I would never allow anything to happen to you. I swear on my life."

"And I believe you'd try with all your might. My want for you frustrates me…it's dangerous and faithless.

As much as I want you…how much I crave your touch. To feel your lips upon my body and to have you inside me…I shouldn't!" She sat up.

"Then why do it? Why disobey your "dominus" and sneak away to have a prohibited encounter with a man you are not supposed to so much as exchange words with? Why involve yourself with me if this is so perilous?"

"Because, you are impossible…" She paused momentarily. *"…impossible to resist and impossible to have."*

I silently gazed into her eyes for a moment. *"But, am I impossible to love?"*

With a hard swallow, Susurri gathered her clothing and began dressing herself unresponsively.

"Answer me!" I begged.

Hiking up her shorts, Susurri reached out to grab the entrance zipper. *"No… you are not."*

Pulling my jeans up and over my ass, I sat cradling my head within my hands. Why did this shit have to be wrong or impossible? It wasn't—it was just difficult. Because love isn't easy, it never has been.

Throwing my shirt and cut back on, I opened the door and who other than Benjamin himself to be the one standing several feet away with a deathly stare through blackened eyes.

His gaze remained fixated as if he were

withdrawing the very soul from within me. I wasn't sure if he had seen Susurri run off from here, or if he just resented me that damn badly. Either way, the man has never welcomed me with a comforting smile and a warm embrace and I doubted there would ever come a day in which he would.

I made my way back to where Adam was passed out in a fold out chair—beer still in hand. I gently pulled it from his grasp, tossing it into the fire before waking him up.

"Adam, let's go find a place to rest. I'm tired and if I drink anymore, my liver is going to dissolve inside me."

Adam cracked a half coherent smile while getting up to follow me. He guided me over to a place he had set up earlier beneath a tree. A few blankets were sprawled out neatly and untouched. Dropping to his knees, Adam nestled down finding a comfortable position to lie.

"Get some sleep, kid. We have to get up and do it all again tomorrow."

I felt sarcastically overjoyed as I lied on my back counting stars until my eyes became heavy.

****

The following day...

I felt a hard kick to my ribcage as I groaned to awaken. Rolling over, I squinted to find my surroundings as the sun's rays burned against my face.

"Get the fuck up. You and Kian are running the beer booth to earn us some extra money." Benjamin's voice carried.

Not the way I wanted to wake up after drinking all night, but what else could I really expect? Hundreds of bikers were scattered about the premises celebrating the purpose of our supported charity.

I met up with Kian and positioned myself underneath a tent with our club's name printed into the canvas. With no words thrown my way, Kian kept to himself passing out beer to the early birds. Something was different about him, as if he were proud or swayed to the dark side by Moira's persuasive cunt.

"Why the fuck you smiling like that for?"

Kian snapped his head in my direction, drawing his brows together. *"Like what?"*

"I don't know? That's why I'm asking you, dummy. You two fucked, didn't you?"

He just gave a shrug with a subtle laugh. *"Between us... you already know, brother."*

I shook my head almost with disgust. *"That bitch will fuck anything with a swinging pulse."*

Polished nails clutching a red solo cup stretched out before me. My eyes moved up toward her face to see a woman from another bike club. Holding an innocent gaze with an inviting smile, the woman slid her sunglasses to the top of her head to give me a more personable glance. She couldn't have been much older than me, standing in a white leather jacket and tight jeans that fit like a glove. Her light caramel hair flowed free from restraint and lied past her shoulders without a bend to any strand. Mahogany eyes held me prisoner with the twinkle of stratagem flickering in her dark expression.

I filled her cup by the tap, but never parted eyes. Over her shoulder, I spotted Susurri standing with Moira and Renny; marring a silent intone of displeasure. I looked back at the woman standing before me as she touched my hand while drawing the cup back.

Leaning forward into my ear, she placed a hundred dollar bill into our tip jar. *"Gratias."*

Never knowing what most of these people are up to...whatever scandals they seem to plot; I grabbed her arm before she could leave. *"What are the intensions behind your generosity?"* My face remained straight.

"Nothing beyond genuine courtesy..." She smirked. *"Prospect."*

My eyes glanced down at the prominence of perky breasts set tight beneath her undershirt. *"Easton..."*

"...Dahlia." She replied sweetly.

Something so mysterious about her pulled out a deep curiosity. Though the look I received from Susurri wasn't one of endearment. Moira immediately headed towards the tent no sooner than Dahlia had stepped away.

"Careful Easton...we aren't to mingle with outsiders—especially a proditor." She sneered.

"You're always so good at finding the worst in others...what has Dahlia ever done to you?"

"Oh, we are on a first name basis already? What a slick black widow she is." She laughed tauntingly.

My nerves irked the more mordant and caustic her attitude became. *"Yes, we exchanged first names. That's generally how humans communicate."* I snapped.

"Ooh...Easton, so sexy when those pale blue eyes darken with aggression. To save a long story, Dahlia used to be property of our club until she met another rider at one of these shindigs about two years ago."

"Who did she belong to?"

Moira arched an eyebrow to my sudden interest. *"Chad..."*

"Why did she leave?"

"Because, Chad used to beat the shit out of her! So in sheer rebellious rage, pretty little Dahlia ventured

out to becoming a member of the Revolting Pixies. It is a rather pathetic patch to bear in my opinion, but she wanted freedom to ride and do as she pleases… so they offered her a probation period to prospect and she took them up on their generous offer."

"Chad just let her go like that?"

"Not without one hell of a fight. My God, it was glorious! The moment Chad watched her hop off of another man's bike he ran full speed at the guy and beat him to the ground. He left the man with three broken ribs, a busted nose, a broken cheek bone and a dislocated kneecap. I have never seen Chad so outraged before then. He didn't want probation so he served a year and a day in prison for aggravated assault with deadly force. He's lucky that's all he received."

"I can see why he beat the fuck of that guy…" My words trailed off.

"Don't get any ideas in that thick head of yours, Easton. You belong to us…let us not forget."

I drew in a harsh breath, scooping up a bottle of beer. Popping its top, I downed the entirety within seconds before crushing the bottle in my grasp. Kian's eyes widened once the crackly pop echoed in the air, but he didn't dare ask what was wrong.

"Not to pour salt in the wound…but why do you let her get to you so much?"

"Because she knows how to." I clenched my jaw.

Within the hour, my eyes captured pretty little
Dahlia striding effortlessly through the crowd before
me, clinging to the arm of another female rider from
her club. I felt worry nestle in my gut seeing Benjamin
standing with Chad and Ryder in the corner of my right
eye. Brave and bold, it was as if she knew he'd be
present. But fear didn't shadow her newly experience of
freedom as she waltzed right before Chad's view. Not so
much in a flaunty 'look at me now' kind of way, but a
confident strut that would turn any man's head if they
had caught a glimpse.

Benjamin yelled some rude obscene slander
directing it towards her and the members that grouped
alongside as she laughed only to stop dead in her tracks.
I nudged Kian to pay attention to the boiling conflict
that was arising before us. With an arrogant shrug of
the shoulders, Chad stalked his way over to where she
was standing as if nothing was going to dare try and
stop him.

Running a hand through his dirty blonde hair,
Chad bared a large smile before licking his lips. I
imagined it had been quite some time since they have
seen one another. Opening his arms wide for a hug,
Dahlia placed a hand to his chest—shoving away his
offer. Taking offense, he released a cocky chuckle
pulling her in by the hips with a sexual gesture.

Closing in the space between their bodies, Chad
leaned in to whisper in her ear. I could see history
familiarize harmony between them, but the way he tried
to take control of her in front of everyone was a bit
overbearing. He had been drinking, I could tell by the

redness in his pigmentation, but that has never stopped him from doing what he wanted. As much as I wanted to tell him to step off, the instant reminder of the lashes placed upon my back had me rooted to the soil.

He wanted her—I could tell. The radiance of testosterone was enough to prick my stomach from its overexertion of power. The way his hands reached back to cup voluptuous cheeks perked up by Levis and the pulse beneath his skin as it ticked with eagerness of eruption just to have her against him. Maybe he truly missed her, I couldn't tell you with just the little knowledge I recently carried of the two and their past.

Dahlia seemed uninterested, but fought to resist the fever rush he may have given her at one point in time. Chad took both of her hands and placed them against his large chest as he stood stout, yearning for more. I could read the gloss of wetted lips as she repeatedly asked him to stop. The ache inside nearly had his chest explode with each attempt she made to jerk away from his grasp.

Benjamin and Ryder stood by without intervening, allowing the two to hash out whatever unresolved business Chad and Dahlia may have had. Taking my attention away from the live soap opera, Adam shoulder bumped me with a rugged sigh.

"Those two right there are combustible." He chuckled.

"How do you mean?"

"They were just horrible together. I'm glad she got away for her sake. Chad was crazy for her, but to the point he became overprotective in the wrong way—kind of obsessive. He'd gouge the eyes of any man who was caught staring. I remember one day at the clubhouse, everyone was hanging out throwing the bull and having a good time when Chad had a little too much to drink and mistook another member's offer in getting Dahlia another. The sight of him placing his hand on the small of her back had Chad fly from his seat and slam the guy's head right off the bar, knocking him out."

"Jesus Christ!"

"Yeah, he was very serious about Dahlia. She was everything to him. The day she left was the day he lost his mental. I'd never want to get caught alone in an alleyway with him. That bull has so much pent up anger, he just doesn't know when to quit."

"If she meant so much, why did he beat her like he did?"

"Did Moira tell you that?" He rolled his eyes.

I gave him an uncharacterized glare as he went on. *"I honestly couldn't tell you what his problem was. I know they were each other's first love and they were always caught messing around when we had other club business going on. Then Chad began drinking an awful lot after losing his father in a horrible bike accident."*

"So, instead of embracing her comfort...he used her as a fucking human punching bag? That's ridiculous!"

"Half the time, I don't think he even knew what he was doing. We all knew what was going on, but everyone was "hush hush" about it—especially Ryder and Benjamin. Those two would kill for Chad without any questions asked. It tore him to pieces when Dahlia chose to leave, of course we couldn't stop her. I didn't blame her one bit, although Chad is permanently bitter after the fact, we still love him just the same."

Jerking free from his hands, Dahlia looked in my direction as if she dared me to save her. Those bounds I knew all too well not to cross, no matter how badly I'd love to indulge in the innocence of a broken heart with an imperfect shield. I watched her walk off leaving him alone and damaged just the same he had once left her.

We never really know how to handle certain situations or how they are going to affect us. We can be trained hours on end on how to deal with life, how to control our emotions and let things go. Then the clincher comes with the one thing only you know that can possibly defeat you...and well instinctively, you let it. –Weaknesses.

Sixteen

I once had a vision, one in which my brothers would come to the conclusion of what peace really valued—how it even felt. I claimed to withhold strength and control in the vacancy of my mind instead of extricating accumulated skills to defend humanity. Fear is one of many emotions we contain and practice regularly. It distresses while finding unwanted comfort in provoking impendence of danger. We all carry the propensity to embrace its reverential radiation without having the admittance of acceptance to its evil nature.

Although, terror carries intimidation coercing our curiosity to take an action towards the unknown, I believe love holds the highest position; daunting through the iron cage that is bolted inside our chest. To love another is much easier than it is to love ourselves. We are our biggest fans…yet, we are our worst and most crucial critic. No matter the confidence one carries, we all allow the simplest of flaws to devour our own dignity.

How dare we judge another for not appreciating the life granted to them? What we don't understand is that it isn't the life we lead, the beat within our breast, or the blood coursing rapidly through our veins. It's the breath we breathe that is taken for granted. It is so natural that we never have to stop and count the seconds between each inhale. Most people don't know what it really means to breathe—we've forgotten.

You may ask, how can we possibly forget an autonomic function molted into the depths of our medulla oblongata? Well, because humans are programed to sustain actions that keep our organism secure and living. We however, are not intended to possess the natural inhabitance of shutting out the normality of developed feelings. Suddenly, something is supposedly clinically wrong with our powerhouse; we are then maimed as the poster child for what is considered to be a psychopath or sociopath.

Whether we accept how we feel and solidify our personal opinion towards a situation…we are still human beings that have the power to control our actions—even if it means to simply forget how to stop and take a proper moment to breathe. Should we really shame ourselves for unintentional neglect?

I twisted whitened rived fabric down inside a glass stange in the overbearing silence of the clubhouse. Kian was busy restocking the cooler while everyone else was either outside or off on a business ride. I wasn't forced to go on their venture of illegal activity, but I was completely content with the fact.

A cool zephyr blew through the doorway surrounding the presence of the unexpected. I felt my gaze sharpen as those tight legs my waist longed for strode across the hardwood—heels clacking to each thud my heart extruded.

Arching an intrepid brow with a devious smile, Susurri reached her hand out taking the glass from my grasp. I wetted my lips trying to force the lump down my throat, feeling myself harden like cement. Darting her eyes towards the back hallway, I shattered my hesitance with brisk steps to catch up.

Peering down the dimmed hallway, the silhouette illuminating desire stood before Ryder's office door. As if the devil himself led me by the hand, I hurried in—shutting the door swiftly behind me.

Reaching forward to grab ahold of Susurri's hips, I slid my fingers down into the recess of her v-cut, pressing my groin against her ass. Falling back against me, I felt her hands take a vice grip to the thighs of my jeans the more pressure my fingers had applied. An inarticulate sigh escaped Susurri's mouth as she pulled her hands to mine, gripping me as her knees began to weaken.

Stiffening the tips of my fingers, I dragged them up beneath her shirt, waving over each rib until my hands met fabricated wire. Penetrating both index fingers for access, I lifted upward reaching in both yearning palms to cup soft, perky breasts that elevated nervously.

Bowing my head downward, I placed the roughness of my face flush against her cheek as a rugged groan trailed into her ear. I wanted her against me more than the life that clung sparingly to my soul.

"Are you sure about this?" I asked, stuck in a trance.

Turning to face me, she smiled. *"I have always been sure about you."* A deep exhale escaped her mouth. *"The only thing I have ever been sure of since I can remember."*

"If you feel so passionately to always condone your place, why is it you stay?"

"You just answered your own question. This is my place, whether I disobey the bylaws or not."

Tracing the pads of my thumbs against the softness of her jawline, I placed my lips to her forehead before beginning an interval of light kisses. *"You belong right here within my embrace. Not beneath the hammer of a man who knows not a damn thing about you."*

"He knows me…just not in the way you do."

"Susurri…" I tipped her chin upward to meet my eyes. *"I would always promise to love you fiercely, vow to always protect you and ensure that your happiness is to always come before anything else."*

A shined layer glossed over her eyes as she attempted to swallow her tears. *"I know…"* She whispered. *"It has been said that forbidden love is the strongest."*

"But it isn't overpowered by faith, itself."

Hearing the jiggling of the door handle, my eyes shot towards its direction as my heartbeat accelerated. I couldn't run, I could no longer hide. Though the dilation of Susurri's pupils offered a safe place to climb into for protection, the sight of Moira's demonic grin appeared on the other side. The door flung completely open as Benjamin's boot nearly kicked it from the hinge.

Two days ago...

My mind rested in a numbed paramnesia as I stared down at a business card inscribed with the Revolting Pixies club information. Kian claimed it was found at the bottom of our tip jar. Why he gave it to me, I will probably never know.

I glanced over the top of my teacup as streams of vapor set my eyes to water. Lemon tickled my pallet with a citrus zest leaving a tingle sensation over the smooth of my lips.

My mother knelt down in a practiced manner, resting corduroy decorative knees firmly in the grass while gliding floral gloves through fresh soil. Her straw brim flopped loosely above her face, presenting an indolent shield against threatening ultraviolet.

Remaining so silent, dwelling in therapeutic tranquility harmonizing with the swarming vultures picking the fragments of her mind one day at a time. Past imposed injuries ached and twitched through my muscles, trailing a steady burn into the core of my marrow. It hurt me more to know I'd lose my mind if something were to ever happen to my mother. A woman so innocent and carefree, yet vigorous and protective— she doesn't deserve further pain, especially inflicted by her own son.

My eyes danced over the swaying branches leading in an old beat up GTO with my best mate hanging his left arm outside the driver's window. Stepping out to place his boots into the gravel, Draper tugged at the waist of his jeans for adjustment having sat down for so long. A generous wave was directed towards my mother as he emerged towards the front porch. I listened in on their subtle conversation about how my mother believes he should make it a point to come around more often. I think she just misses watching two fearless and resilient towheads running around the yard with cardboard swords and pillow cases tied comfortably around our tiny necks.

When I first started with the corps, my mother would always write to me explaining how she felt she had developed 'empty nest' syndrome. Silly things like that were what got me through while I was over a thousand miles away from her embrace. If I had to be quite honest, I would much rather have re-enlisted, spending countless hours on night watch as opposed to being enslaved by ruthless rebels who would rather have me dead.

Tremors waved through my being as Draper's arms wrapped tightly around the fragile frame that stood nearly a foot and a half shorter. Parting to allow her to continue on, long legs strode in my direction clacking pointed cowhide up the steps with a large smile illuminating his greeting.

"Hey, I got your message. Is everything all right?" He smirked with uncertainty.

I motioned for him to take the available seat beside me, watching his brows draw together. *"I have a proposition for you. You don't need to fall under the pressure of obligation, either. It's just a suggestive offer. Maybe even a plea for help in my expense."*

Worry controlled his expression as a question formulated in his mind, so obvious he chose not to ask. *"Anything I can do to help a brother out. Shoot."*

I felt myself mirror his inviting smile, gazing into a whitened mouth of perfected rows of teeth. *"I know how strongly you feel about my affiliation with this bike club I have been held captive by. But, I feel something horrible is bound to happen…and well, it's my own damn fault anyhow."* The purpose of my rant trailed off as my mind became pierced with a thought of Susurri.

"It isn't that I am an activist against your choices, I just don't fully comprehend why you want to do this with your life? I know you, Easton. This shit…it isn't you." He shook his head.

"That's just it…it isn't my choice. It never was." I could see the wheels begin to rotate the more I explained. *"That night at the bar has changed my life."*

"I read in the paper that that guy ended up dying. You don't honestly blame yourself for that, do you? You were only protecting yourself. Is this whole biker thing some act of rebellion? Or some prognostic belief that being one of them grants you repentance?"

"No. It's nothing like that. I was literally forced to prospect for these guys or else…" I paused, taking a long gander at my mother spraying mist across the garden.

"…Or else what?" He begged to regain my attention.

My eyes landed directly on his. *"They were going to kill me."*

Large with horror, his bottom jaw lowered as he troubled to find a response. *"How can you get out of it? Certainly, there must be a way!"*

"There would have been if I wasn't "forced" into it. It isn't like being a part of a sports team and when

you've had enough they let you quit, or even a job…they retire you with graceful hands. This is a born to kill lifestyle."

"Then, what the hell do you want me to do? I feel a bit defeated here."

"Be there for me. Have my back like a brother would."

That same familiar smile with easy eyes stretched across his face. *"If we fall, we fall together."* He reached over taking ahold of my shoulder.

Later on down at the clubhouse, everyone was busy bitching about the money that was raised at the event. Of course, no amount was ever enough nowadays. Stacking shot glasses into obnoxious pyramids, Kian stood next to me behind the bar with a blank expression. Quickly to change his attitude, Moira came waltzing up with a malicious grin. Plopping down onto a barstool, she looked at Kian with a smile while running her hands over his—only to drop into a frown once her eyes met mine.

"So, are you two like a "thing" now?" I asked sarcastically.

"At least we can be…publically." Moira shot back.

My posture straightened as my face sealed over like stone. *"How nice? I bet you feel privileged being his bitch."* My eyes flickered towards the Budweiser clock hanging over the doorway.

As expected and always on time no matter the occasion, Draper stepped through the opening pulling his shades from his face while taking a long look around.

Following my eyes, Moira slid around the stool immediately lowering to her feet. Draper's eyes darted towards mine, but only for a brief moment until locking his stare in on Ryder who was staring right back.

I sat back watching the magic begin to play out as Draper played his part oh so well with a fabricated authentic leather vest clutching to his torso with our club patch stitched into the back. Being a pre-med student who majored in Latin... who else could I have possibly asked for help?

"Can I help you?" Benjamin moved in his direction with a pool stick vulnerable within his grip.

"I'm from Chapter 13 up in Kentucky. I was in the area and figured I could step into a nearby home for a rest period."

Benjamin studied his behavior while Ryder stepped forward with an unexpected welcome. *"Mitescere, Benjamin. The man is proclaimed family."* He glanced over Drapers cut. *"Are you a recent member?"*

"How recent do you think?" Draper began a level of reverse psychology.

Chad stepped forward, baring two metal darts in his right hand. *"I'd say pretty fucking recent."* His voice tightened. *"Your patches lack fray and washout from the sun."*

My gaze sharpened as Moira strode very elegantly in Draper's direction; arms stretched out behind with her fingertips locked in a childish manner. Looking him over, a silence ensued as Moira ran her hand up his back, gliding it down his arm to rest on his bicep. Snatching him by the left wrist, her eyes darted downward to traditional ink sponsoring the clubs symbol.

I felt the breath fall from my mouth as I knocked over a mug rested beside my left elbow. Foamed gold spilled across the bar top, but my eyes couldn't pull away from what was happening before me. I could see Kian throw a rag over the puddle in my peripheral as I mentally nodded with a thank you.

Moving her hands to his beltline, Moira gradually slid her hands slowly around his hips, pulling him in to close the space between them. His unwavering gaze had her nip at her bottom lip as a subtle laugh escaped her mouth. Pulling her right hand back, a black 21 A Bobcat berretta was gripped in her grasp. With a reveling smile, she released the clip before cocking the slide back to unload it. I'd be lying if I said I wasn't enjoying the way she taunted the supposed 'outsider reeking of fresh meat'.

Placing a golden bullet in between her teeth, a light click echoed into the air thickened with inquisitive wonder. Slightly lowering her bottom jaw, the bullet fell to the floor with a clink.

"You will not need this while you're in our house." She handed it off to Benjamin as he studied its makeup. Leaning in closer to his face, her hand slid to the front of his jeans. *"The only bullet that shall penetrate anyone will be shot from the pistol between your legs…"* She tightened her grip with a sigh.

Draper released a grunt through his nostrils, removing her hand. *"Let's not get ahead of ourselves, miss. I am only visiting."* He shot her a confident wink.

Practically melting her heart, she clutched her chest gushing in his presence. *"Innoxius."* She waved over her shoulder before walking off.

"I'm still going to keep my eye on you…" Benjamin followed up.

"Maxime." Draper returned a smile.

It had been nearly twenty minutes since I stopped breathing normally. But, I figured Draper had everything under control. I finished cleaning up the spilt beer while Draper shook hands with his enemy. Having entered the lion's den without hesitation, I could only hope his purpose remained solid as concrete.

"To continue business, tomorrow we have a nice haul to our Chapter 18 in Nashville." Ryder went on.

Coming up to the bar, Draper mastered a poker face. *"All right, pour me a hard shot ya prospect fuck."* He said with amusement.

Pouring up a shot of aged Bushmills, I slid the glass into his palm with annoyance. *"Don't overdo it."* I said through gritted teeth.

Giving a shrug, Draped downed the shot without a blink of an eye. Curious about our friendly engagement, Adam side-stepped in our direction; casually sipping the foam from the top of his mug.

"You two had better not make it too noticeable."

"Whatever do you mean?" Sarcasm flowed from Draper's mouth.

"That you two are in acquaintance with one another…" Watching members walk by talking amongst one another, Adam continued a steady conversation. *"You had better make sure the people you two are involving in your madness are loyal to the core. If this shit goes wrong, we are all fucked! I give you my word that I respect your outlook on wanting to change things around here, but it's a longshot in the damn dark. Keep it kosher and as planned."*

"Okay, now I'm confused." I drew my brows together. *"What "madness" are you insinuating?"*

"Do you not remember explaining this entire scheme to me the other night? We had a long conversation before you passed out drunk."

I stood for a moment trying to jog my memory of the past few days. Everything seemed to portray a blur as I struggled to remember a damn thing. My frozen gaze shattered as Susurri walked within my line of vision, breaking my concentration. Maybe I had made the mistake of explaining the plot of insanity, though I wish he had assumed I was talking shit while under the influence. He must know me better...holy shit—Adam actually knows me.

"If you believe whatever I had supposedly spilt that night, why is it you haven't turned me in to the board?"

Adam belted out a ridiculous laugh. *"Because, I am ready to see these fuckers get some. If it means to cradle them while on their way to hell, then I will do whatever it takes. By the way, I'm Adam—the club's secretary."* He reached out his hand towards Draper.

"The only advice I can give you is to be weary of your surroundings." I suggested.

"I did my research. I know what is expected. Besides, I did a thesis on these guys my freshman year for one of my classes."

The rumble of bikes came pulling up out front, causing everyone to file out the door. Two other females from the Revolting Pixies hopped off their bikes following Dahlia's lead. A laugh jammed in my throat seeing Chad's expression—jaw to the floor, nearly trembling at the knees.

Sporting punk rock ankle boots, a sole perched up by three inches with pyramid studs lining the secure straps over the black laces ended below tight, form fitting ash black skinny jeans that comfortably hugged defined hips. Diamond rhinestones and silver iron crosses twinkled in my sight as my eyes rose to a black skin tight tank top with transparent mesh fabric showing off a taut lower abdomen and a thin strip diagonally across the top of her right breast leading to the bottom of the left for a visual arousing tease. Thick, black fabric covered the exciting parts, but left just enough to have every man out here pitching a damn tent.

Smooth caramel strands lied neatly behind her shoulders as she ran a hand through to push them from her face. Not caring to give anyone else her attention, Dahlia awaited Chad to come forth and approach her. What a way to play a dirty game…there's never a rule against using a sweet vixen to entice a hungry wolf.

Nobody moved…no one exchanged words—they stood on guard, heeding their master's command to pause. I could hear Draper's gnaw on a toothpick intensify as his eyes locked in on a woman we barely knew anything beyond a first name. Standing with a reign of confidence, not shaken by evil eyes piercing her appearance, fearless to a former homeland that suffocated beneath her heels—she was powerful.

Whispers leaked into the awkward air causing tension to arise in the reddened neck rested beneath a tattered cut worn through many winds of weather.

Flicking his infamous blade open digging dirt from beneath his nails, Benjamin leaned against the wall of the clubhouse bending one knee up. *"You had better handle this shit, Chad. Or we will…"*

Knowing no one is allowed on the premises without permission, or a vouch from a full-patched member, Chad nervously made his way towards his former lover. I could almost see his knees weaken the closer he'd become—her eyes never moving from him.

Chills cruised down my spine feeling their chemistry radiate through the atmosphere as everyone stood in silent awe.

"Why have you come back, Dahlia? You've made your treacherous decision long ago. I'm quite sure we all have put a possible return to rest." Ryder adduced.

Raising his left hand in a submissive request to allow him to continue conversation alone, Chad struggled to speak further.

"He is right, why have you come back? To watch me fall to my knees as you choose to leave again? To clutch my tainted heart with glorious might because you can?"

"Stop it…" Dahlia made her best attempt to contain her composure.

"You know the rules, Dahlia. You should not be here."

Closing the space between them, Dahlia pulled him in by the flaps of his cut peering directly at me over his shoulder. *"Vouch for me then, Chad. If I didn't want to be surrounded by your arrogance shrouded by your little "Napoleon syndrome", I doubt I'd be standing here breathing the same air."*

Taking his hands to that tight ass Dahlia carried with advantage, Chad pressed her pelvis against his. *"So, you do miss me."* A self-assertive grin pulled up his cheeks.

"Let's not jerk at the throttle too hard, baby." She giggled. *"Just an FYI, it's open house, as it has been scheduled for many years on your goddamn calendar."* Stepping away, Dahlia slid her shades down to cover her eyes.

"What makes you think I even want you here?" He turned to face everyone. *"Who else would vouch for you and those little bitches upholding your pedestal? I am not enthralled."* He said smugly.

Dahlia's eyes narrowed in on her prey. *"Don't make me show you just who would grant me passage, Chad. Do you really want to see these men have me before your very eyes? Crumble inside as you witness me being pounded by severe penetration, holding me against my will because, ha—we all know they'd love to."* Her mouth clamped shut with her conclusion.

His faced pinched with bitterness, flaring his nostrils like the riled bull he yearned to release. Turning to slowly face everyone once again, Chad lowered to one knee placing his right fist over his chest. *"I take claim over these women, granting permission to enter our sanctuary. I am responsible for all that they do, whether right or wrong, I will be held accountable and will be handled appropriately. With these words, I promise to uphold the bylaws of my brotherhood. For they come first. Semper!"*

I have never witnessed how one asks permission to allow another rider in, but it was so precise and organized. Like a written law one must always obey, bowing to the king of their land.

"Chad…" Benjamin paused.

"No, I allow them to come in. It is open house, as she proclaimed." Ryder intervened.

"But, you all must take off your colors. I don't want a disgrace such as some dainty "pixies" emasculating the damn clubhouse." Benjamin snarled as he shoved his knife deep into his pocket.

"How the fuck did Dahlia find out? She would have never set another foot here, otherwise." I turned towards Draper.

"Remember that purple and black business card you had been all but disintegrated in your fingertips? I took it and looked them up. They are not 1%ers, Easton. Yes, granted they are a tough club, but they do not practice the same bylaws as the Disciples do."

"Well, what was the point in bringing her in?"

"I offered her a generous proposal and now that I have seen her in person, I surly hold no regret." He chuckled. *"She explained her history with these guys and gave me the incentive that she is as dangerous as a damn atomic bomb. She knows the ins and outs, she knows what is to be expected while present and she has great sex appeal and attraction empowerment over one of your leaders."*

"You are so damn clever." I found it hard to keep from smiling.

"Hence the "pre-med"." Draper joked. *"The other women she brought with her are road guides and/or captains, if you will. They concealed cocaine to smuggle it in. I also found out that your organization in this particular area does not tolerate the trafficking, manufacturing, or usage of the drug. But, they do traffic very subtly with women as sex figures or "clubhouse meretricum". Which is precisely why that pretty little pistol used knowledge for advantage to gain entry. They do not want their business spread about, but your sub-division answers to the big guys up north. A man by the name of Maebeck runs that house and the rest down this way."*

"I know who he is. I had to make a falsified delivery to him once." I felt disgusted.

"Since we all know we are not supposed to deal with the product, the Pixies brought enough to place

small doses and traces throughout the club. Ryder's desktop, the cooler maybe? I left the locations up for them to decide."

"So, that's it? That's your master plan, to place cocaine all over the damn clubhouse?"

"Absolutely! One tiny bug placed in Ryder's superior's ear, they will tear the paint from asphalt to come down here and handle it. You have not been around these guys for but a month. There's a lot of underground shit you have yet to discover."

My mind reveled in the semi-perfect scheme; it just needed my twist of genius competence dripping with spiteful acid. What was a better way to get caught just to show how beastly vicious these men were. To shine light upon their unfavorable ways to long ranged hierarchy. I had to place the danger on me; I had to make them see me. Question me not with fear, but wondrous delusion. Like Adam always told me, 'how are they to fear us if we never show ourselves?' You've got to make them believe you are the baddest kid on the playground; you must control the rattled terror caving the chests of your audience. We all possess the nature of wanting to feel a little bit of power. If we master the proper usage, the greatest of events are awaiting.

Watching Dahlia and her deadly entourage divide and conquer, I sat back formulating my own revenge. For quite some time, Chad didn't dare move towards Dahlia. He only watched her—in the way I watched Susurri. How she's leaned up against the pool table laughing and carrying on with Moira, as always. How her smile can affect anyone by stopping them dead in their tracks. How it was killing me inside just to be able to speak to her freely, to touch her publically and effortlessly.

Heels that clack to match my heartbeat, eyes with a deep set gaze that weakened my knees every glance she threw my way. How her touch raised every tiny hair on my body, sending never-ending chills beneath my skin. She gives a rush, promising to implode internally from an overabundance of excitement. I have never wanted someone so badly in my entire life, not even as bad to see my father again. She had my heart— and she had it from day one. I was ready to fight and take control, breaking free from my shell of fear. I should not be punished for something my heart refuses to find an ending point. I am a man, I have always known what I've wanted—and I was certain to claim what belonged with me.

Hours into the night of obnoxious noise and drunken members stumbling about, I kept a wary eye on every move my targets made. I was slowly becoming overly intoxicated to where my mind became clouded. Seated beside Adam at a small poker table, I tried ignoring the ache in my bladder that was on the verge of busting.

"I'll be right back." I nudged Adam in the arm.

Teetering down the back hallway, I shoved my way into the restroom. Planting a hand against the wall,

I barely had enough time to pull down my zipper before piss exploded onto the urinal's porcelain. The privacy walls of the handicap stall were rocking as a woman's pleasurable moans echoed. I should have just walked out, but a man's curiosity led me to investigate. The door was closed and locked—of course. I squinted through the crack looking my best friend in the back as he rammed into some chick. I understood that he wanted to 'blend in", but goddamn!

I quickly washed my hands, yanking a paper towel before exiting. Plopping back down to overlook a game of Texas Hold em', I pulled my glass of Redbreast on the rocks to my face for a hard chug. Turning my direction to Kian behind the bar conversing with a member from the Pixies, my eyes landed on Draper coming from the back hallway with Dahlia following right behind. I felt myself begin to choke on my own saliva as they inconspicuously parted ways.

Nearing my direction, I knew he'd seen the flushness of my face. *"Hey, I'm going to get outta here for the night. Got some "paperwork" due tomorrow."* He winked with a hardy slap to my shoulder.

Standing to my feet, I pulled Draper in for a hug. *"Let's not forget our purpose."*

Pulling away with furrowed brows, he searched my eyes for meaning behind my remark. I flicked my eyes towards the bar where Dahlia was seated. He followed my motion with a hard swallow only to quickly look away.

"Can I not have a little fun?" He smirked with charm.

"You are not to be seen speaking with her…much more fucking her! If you had done your research a little more in depth then you would know that!" I bit out.

Noticing gaining eyes, Draper hauled me towards the front door before we were overheard. *"Damnit, Easton. I know what I am doing! I got a fucking tattoo that is permanent just to help you and you're going to scold me over a piece of ass?"*

"It isn't just that…I don't want or need you distracted. It isn't like we can really trust any of these people, now can we? Any bitch here will throw their cunt just to get what they want. Trust me…I've learned the hard way."

Placing a hand on his hip, tracing his five o'clock shadow, Draper became skeptical. *"Are you telling me that you are involved with one of these females?"*

I pressed my lips together inhaling through my nostrils. With bewilderment, Draper took his hands through his hair in disbelief. *"No way, man! Who is she? She that scandalous bitch "Moira?" Come on, tell a brother!"*

"No… someone more dangerous."

He took a second to think. *"Are you fucking with Ryder's ol' lady? Holy sweet baby Jesus, Easton!"*

"Shh! Hush your damn trap before you have us both skinned."

"That must be exciting!" He beamed. *"You are fucking ballsy, man. I would never attempt that shit…never in a million years."* He paused to study my face. *"You know that will get you killed, right?"* He became worried.

"I know all too well of its consequences."

"Then why continue?" His voice rose.

"Because, when you love someone you'd do anything for them."

Suckling at his top lip beneath the giant street light, Draper stood in deep consideration. *"Listen, I have always envied your courage, your strength to just look evil in the eye and say "fuck you" and how fearless you have always stood to be. I admire the fuck out of you and there has never been a time I haven't had your back on something, no matter how insane I thought you were. I—I love ya, man. You're the brother I never had and my life wouldn't have turned out the way it has if you ceased to ever become a part of it."*

"All right now, don't you be going soft on me. I love ya, too. You're a great guy, but honestly…you went and got a permanent fucking tattoo?"

Draper playfully shoved me as we laughed our asses off like we had when we were younger.

Seventeen

A day ago...

It was clammy and the air settled thick before
the high set moon. I felt I had had enough with
torturing myself all evening, watching harsh hands
glide all over the tight body that bared my marking.

Pulling up to my home, the porch light was not burning, but my mother's car sat in the very distinctive tracks it always had.

Something was unusual, the way I felt was eerie and perhaps a bit frightening. So many dramatic scenarios were flashing through my mind, leading me into direct paranoia. Walking up towards the front porch I drew my pistol, slowly cocking the slide back. The click of a bullet entering the chamber sent a pricking quiver through my skin. I found myself entering my home as I would an unfamiliar building in the middle of a night scout. Flicking on the kitchen light, the room quickly settled in my vision. I know my house by square inch; I know where everything is and its exact position. Nothing is ever moved, misplaced, or relocated. For the sake of my mother's dissolving memory, everything was kept in the same place for assistance—to lesson possible confusion.

My mother became so overwhelmed last week making a trip to the grocery store, my neighbor claimed she thankfully knew his number in that moment and gave him a call. How does that even happen? As the knife twists in further, knowing my jackass wasn't there to hold her hand—to guide her in the right direction. How shitty of her own pathetic flesh and blood to leave her unintentionally stranded, alone…even scared. I never received a missed call from her, then again how is she to remember her son when he can hardly recognize his own reflection anymore? I am not the same man I was over a month ago. I appear different not just in apparel, but my eyes alone do not see the way they used to. Always overlooking the bigger things just to simply focal in on the finer details. 'Nothing wrong with that', my instructor always told me. Maybe that was my problem; I had an issue with accepting the very surface of things. I had to pick away the layers, dig deeper and find a reason why; no matter how long it took.

I have obsessed over my losses, feared for what tomorrow brings, even torn from my beliefs, shredded by image only to forget who I once claimed to be. I have never once accepted life for what it was. You live by the sword; you surly die just the same. But if one can make a difference, why cower at the command of duty at a destined opportunity?

Looking over each object distinctively placed around the room, I mentally ensured that nothing was wrong. I ran my fingertips across the counter top, across the coffee pot, over the spice rack and oven coils. Pausing for a moment, my eyes caught the glimpse of a teaspoon lying in the sink. My eyes were then drawn to a small circle of dried coffee with slight moisture in its center rested in the depth of the spoon holder.

"That is unlike her…" I mumbled.

Creeping down the hallway, I quietly listened by my door before shoving it open to find the light switch. Nothing stood on the other side, although I envisioned a fucking serial killer sitting on my bed. Wouldn't you?

I kept my gun pointed while scanning the room from wall to wall. A familiar spice rolled through my nostrils, as if he were still standing near. My jaw tightened as my breathing deepened.

Nothing seemed out of normal until the silent atomic bomb lied atop my bed with a burning fuse. It was a photo—you might ask of whom, exactly? My mother lounging in the shade beneath a tree by a lake we used to go fishing at. My mother in her mid-twenties then, blue jean carpi's with a white cotton tee and her favorite sunhat. I looked to be around six years of age, standing with my left hand rested on her shoulder—half toothless smile with sun touched cheeks. Maybe it wasn't my father who I favored, maybe it was that I adored my mother all the more, but never admitted its level of sensitivity.

I felt anger boil in my stomach as I crumbled the picture in my shaking fist. It is one thing to fuck with me, but no one can threaten my mother and run victorious while still drawing breath. Taking long, purposeful strides back into the kitchen, I ran through each room screaming for a simple answer. She was nowhere; I heard nothing, but continued to scream while frantically searching every foot of the floorplan.

Aggressive shouts and childish stomps turned into throwing objects while cursing into the air.

"You want to fuck with me? You want my wrath… you want to break me, destroying what is left to create your own image of what you think I should be. But, what you have yet to realize is that you have created a monster. It's a little hard to find life in something that is already dead!" My voice was a raspy growl.

I flew back outside seeing the driver's side door to my mother's car open. Crawling out with a yawn, I took off scooping her up into my arms.

"Jesus Christ, ma—where the hell have you been? I was worried sick!" I panted.

"I was supposed to go meet up for bingo and completely forgot the reason why I ended up in the car to begin with. After crying from the inability to remember, I took my dosage and apparently dozed off." She chuckled with embarrassment.

"I'm just glad you're all right." I puffed my chest.

Assisting her into her bedroom for the night, I hung in the doorway until she was settled in. My mother pressed her lips together with cheerful smile.

"What is it?" I asked.

"You are just the greatest son I could have ever asked for. Thank you for always being so amazing."

I choked up some before I could respond, but she understood my meaning.

All night, I lied awake staring into the darkness above. I couldn't sleep—I didn't want to. I knew I had to make a severe and harsh decision of endangerment, but if it meant to keep harm from this house, I was down for the cause no matter the cost.

Soon the sun stretched its rays through my blinds, as I tried to bring feeling back into my numbed limbs. My eyes were heavy with my face scraggly and rough, feeling the coolness of water splash onto my skin. The spiciness of after shave traveled through my flared nostrils; the soulless brute was on his way, had he fallen from grace though he was ready to show what he'd become.

𝔓resent time...

I knew the only way to save us was to have other members vouch and back me up, especially the ones who wanted things to change for the better. I had to present the worst of their behavior for all to see. I needed those who wouldn't dare ignore to see the truth. Turning myself in was too easy...but getting caught was certainly another. Why place myself in such horrible danger? Because I am valor, a United States Marine, and one hell of a survivor. Thou shall not hide from their enemy, but embrace them with the greatest of peculiar intentions.

"Egregium opus, Moira." Benjamin praised. Charging into the room towards me, I moved Susurri behind me. *"I knew this fucking shit was going on!"*

Entering slowly behind Moira was the scariest look I had ever witnessed in Ryder's raging eyes. He cracked each individual knuckle, motioning for Moira to leave.

"Susurri…" He shook his head with a tsk. *"Pudeat te."*

I could feel her shaking behind me as Ryder stepped closer.

"If you knew what was good for you, Easton. You'd move the fuck out of my way."

"Ryder…" Susurri began to speak.

"Shut the fuck up, bitch!" He barked with a slap to her face.

The door reopened with Chad and Quaestor entering; Adam held imprisoned in their grasp.

"Moira claimed he was the only fuck who knew about this little scandal." Chad scoffed.

Benjamin took ahold of my cut yanking me aggressively out of the way. *"He said to move, nequam!"*

I lost my balance, falling over as Benjamin picked Susurri up by the waist only to slam her on top of Ryder's desk. Marching over, Ryder frantically undid her shorts, sliding his hand down inside. As I rose to my feet, Benjamin jerked out a pistol from behind him, pointing it to my chest. I quickly threw my hands up, halting my movement.

"Get the fuck down where you belong, dog." Benjamin gave a swift kick to my groin, sending me to my knees.

Looking at Ryder and Susurri over his shoulder, the intensity between their elongated stare settled extreme worry deep in my gut. Extracting his hand, examining the shine across his fingertips, Ryder pulled in an infuriated snarl through his nostrils striking Susurri across the face once more. *"You dare disrespect me, spit in my face and shame your family to be a goddamn whore? Especially with a disobedient bastard like that!"* He pointed towards me. *"I protect you, take care of your every need, give you entitlement and this is how you repay me?"* He leaned in closer. *"I could have let these men have you a very long time ago. I ask you not to do one thing and you let the temptation fog your integrity and loyalty? You are no better than he is, now are you?"*

Yanking Susurri's shorts down to the floor nearly ripping them apart, Ryder undid his jeans, pressing himself against her. She fought to move but he took a hand to her throat, laying her all the way back.

"Chad, get the fuck over here and hold this ungrateful bitch!"

I dropped my head once she began crying in pain. *"No, you will watch you son of a bitch! Look at the mess you have made…you did this to her! I should have killed you when I had the chance."* Benjamin bit out while snatching my head back.

I couldn't handle watching grown ass men take their turn on such a small, defenseless woman. But, who else could I blame for this but myself? I had no idea how serious these guys were about what they preached—how serious their lifestyle truly was. With each thrust made into her, I felt the wind leave my gut as I struggled to breathe.

"Oh, how I've waited so…long for this." Ryder grunted.

Jerking his belt shut once reaching his release, Ryder motioned for Benjamin and Chad to bind Susurri by the hands, dragging her out of the room. I was soon to follow Adam and Quaestor as we were hauled out into the parking lot. I felt a heavy boot land on my lower back as I fell face first into the dirt.

Benjamin took out his stainless steel Smith & Wesson blade, flicking it open inches away from my face. Ripping open my cut, he placed the blade against the fabric of my shirt, slicing it down the center.

"Get him the fuck up and tie him to the post. Adam will go right beside him."

My hands were bound behind me with rope so tight I felt it burning away the top layer of skin. Stuck on my knees, I watched every member stand outside in reticent shock.

"This bastard has caused us nothing but shame, pain and undeserved grief! He should have been put down the moment he decided to take a life that didn't belong to him! Now, I think it is time we teach him a proper lesson of what a true consequence amounts to."

The air filled with calamity of vindictive shouts and jeering; longing for overdue justice in their eyes. The coolness of his blade pressed against my left peck had me twitch under its intimidation. Pressing in further, I felt the burn settle in my skin as Benjamin began to saw away the label in which they marked me with.

I screamed until my vocals gargled and cut out, leaving tears to fall from my eyes. Peeling the chunk of skin completely off, Benjamin held it victoriously in the air with a loud roar. My eyes opened to see Ryder holding Susurri bound into his grip. I took several punches to my face until blood dripped from my mouth and nose, causing my vision to blur through swollen eyes.

Susurri was forced to once again witness me getting publically punished as several members took their anger out on my body. I even felt my ribs crack as Benjamin dropped a boot into my chest. Slowly emerging closer and closer, Ryder cut the rope from Susurri's wrists, throwing her violently forward. Crashing to the dirt, she found her last ounce of strength to make her way towards me.

Collapsing to her knees, Susurri took her hands to my face, sobbing dramatically. *"I should have never let this happen. This is all my fault and I am regretful beyond words."*

Barely able to breathe, my eyes met hers. *"Stop it…this is not just your actions alone, I should have left it alone like I was told."* I tried to hold back my own emotions. *"…I just couldn't."*

"I believed you when you told me you'd do anything for me…" Susurri sniveled.

I released a subtle sigh, drawing my brows together. *"I would die for you…"*

Scooching closer to place my head into her chest, Susurri began to violently weep. I felt my blood soak into her clothing the tighter she held me.

"He would die for her… Ha! Did everyone hear that? The bastard would die for someone he doesn't have the right to. She will never belong to you and you have had the hardest time in accepting that! Get over it, it's life! You crossed the wrong line, you challenged the wrong people. Now look who you are making suffer for your mistakes in your path of destruction!" Moira snapped.

Pulling Susurri away from me, Chad landed a hard hit against my face as I instantly blacked out.

Cold shards of ice water clashed against my skin as I forced my eyes to peel open. Light rain began to fall as mid-day had already passed. Hearing mild coughs to my left, I turned my hanging head to see Adam barely breathing. I was angry; I was irate and mentally distorted with the way things had turned out. It wasn't supposed to end up this way and I was foolish for believing I could take these guys out; alone.

Arching my back to squeeze my shoulder blades inward, I felt droplets land against the wounded flesh on my pec; simultaneously soothing the raw muscle. I groaned and grimaced at the pain, feeling water drop from my lips.

"Those fuckers…"

"What about them?" Adam said wryly.

"They came into my home…they threatened me with a goddamn photograph!" I bit out. *"They have no idea what is to come…it is me they should fear."*

"It was me…" Adam replied faintly, trying to pant less.

"What was you?" I stopped in thought. *"You came into my house, Adam? What the fuck for?"*

"Because, the only way you were going to pull this off was if I put it in your mind that they were after the one thing you cared for most—your mother. Now that everything is in motion," He looked toward the clubhouse. *"…we wait."*

I had no words; I was shocked that he'd ever think of something so brilliant. He reached into my heart, tearing it from the strings without ever feeling empathy. As if he knew the direction I was going to take this. Adam was more than what these guys branded him with—he was a damn rational life saver; a dark angel in disguise who believed in me and my vision.

I could feel the ground vibrate beneath my knees as the thunder of a dozen motorcycles neared down the highway. Ripping through the parking lot, I saw large Harley's and choppers neatly park in formation. Hopping off his bike first and foremost was Maebeck, himself. Long black hair pulled back into a tight ponytail and a well-groomed, long whiskered goatee. Looking in our direction with a Copenhagen spat to the dirt, Maebeck positioned himself before the door's opening with his half gloved hands rested on his hips.

"Ryder! Get you your punk ass out here, along with your chauvinist wannabe mongrels!" He demanded.

Ryder stepped out with one hand rested over the other, clinging to his belt buckle. *"Maebeck..."* He grinned. *"What a pleasant surprise? What are you doing in our division?"* He reached his hand out for a welcoming shake.

Balling his fist, Maebeck struck Ryder across the jaw. *"Don't be a fucking smartass! You know why I am here and it sure as hell isn't over that rat bullshit you pulled."* He barked.

Rubbing the sore area of his mouth, he snatched his shades from his eyes with irritation. Benjamin lurched forward like an aggressive, well-trained attack dog would. Instinctively, Ryder threw a hand up to stop him, but it only caused unsympathetic laughter to arise from the other chapter members.

"Take me into your office, now." His voice remained serious.

As if Ryder had no idea why the hell Maebeck was so pissed off, in which he shouldn't... considering the fact he'd been set up. Ryder stood out of the way after nearly getting trampled on the way in. A lot of screaming and smashing of objects occurred, but I couldn't really see anything from outside. Once Ryder and Benjamin came out tumbling down the steps and into the dirt, more bikes pulled into the lot.

A smile pulled up my cheeks seeing black and purple patches centered into leather.

"Adam..." I whispered. *"Look who's here."* I looked in his direction, but he didn't respond.

"Why the hell are those caddy bitches here? And why the fuck did I find cocaine in your clubhouse, Huh? You have been dealing within our division, Ryder? Can anybody fucking answer me?" Maebeck yanked out a long barrel .44 Magnum revolver, dying to pull the trigger.

"It must have been planted, sir. We don't distribute drugs here. It's in our goddamn bylaws!"

"Shut the fuck up! You are just like your daddy, always trying to put the blame on others. Well guess what? He isn't here to save you and cover up your fucking mess!"

Pausing in mid-sentence, Maebeck's eyes widened as he drew in the sight of Susurri. Jaw dropping to the sight of blood stained on the inner side of her thighs, black tears streaming down her cracked porcelain and the radiance of forced touch that contaminated her innocent nature. Pulling the hammer back on his revolver, Maebeck pointed it towards Benjamin. *"What...in the fuck is going on here?"* His voice darkened.

"Nothing out of the ordinary?" Ryder reassured.

"Bullshit! There are two men tied to fucking posts nearing their death and my Godchild is bleeding from you animals raping her! Who the fuck is responsible is not the question here, I want to know what the fuck is going on and I want to know now!"

Before anyone could speak, Maebeck fired off a round into Benjamin's leg. With a howl, he collapsed to the ground pressing into his wound.

"Get the fuck over here and get on your knees."

Ryder raised his hands submissively while lowering before him. Maebeck placed his revolver back into his holster, replacing an empty hand with a switchblade. Flinging it open, he grabbed a hold of Ryder's cut. *"I have been waiting since the very moment the club voted you in as President…just to do this."* He dug the blade underneath the fibers of Ryder's club patch. Ripping them off piece by piece, I saw all the respected entitlement and dignity drain from Ryder's face. *"You will not tarnish the Disciples as long as I am still breathing."*

I turned my head to see Chad walking up to Dahlia in the most submissive manner a man could after suffocating with guilt.

"Tell me why these men are tied to a post like some damn road kill." Maebeck asked while walking over to us.

Placing his foot against Adam, he tried nudging him awake. *"Looks as if one of your pets died, Ryder. Christ…Adam, I can only imagine what you got yourself into."* He directed his remark over his shoulder. *"Ardan would be highly disappointed that one of his board members is being treated in such a way."*

"For nothing less than treachery, boss." Ryder did all he could to free himself of guilt.

"Is that so?" He looked back at Adam. *"That's a damn shame."* Slowly drawing his gun, Maebeck fired a shot into Adam's chest to reassure that no life existed and if any still clung to Adam's soul…it was nevermore.

I felt myself jump from the loud bang. One that will never settle right with me, one I could never get used to no matter how many hours Ballintino and I used to spend at the rifle range.

Standing to his feet covered in shame, Ryder held out his pistol; pointing it towards Maebeck's backside. *"You think you can just show up here, pretend to have any notion as to what is really happening, then attempt to play God? Heh…no sir. That's not how it works in my mother fucking division."*

Maebeck quickly turned around to see both Ryder and Benjamin pointing guns in his direction. Unable to make a quick decision, Maebeck fired off a shot into Ryder's gut, taking one to his own from Benjamin. Anguish rushed through his body as he charged for my direction.

"This is all because of you, you fucking bastard! I should have killed you when I had the chance!"

Pointing his gun into my chest, I became squeamish with a flinch when gunshots had my heart skip a beat. Not feeling any pain, I opened one eye to see a motionless Benjamin lying before me. Dahlia stood fearless alongside Susurri; pistols in their clutch.

"This is what you've become? I thank God that I left when I did because honestly, I would probably be fucked up—if not dead!" Dahlia exclaimed.

No one moved, as if they were marbleized in their petrified expressions. Even Chad stood defenseless before the victorious women who once obeyed under the title of possession.

"When you left us, you fucked our world up, Dahlia. I used to want to be like you! Perfect life, perfect romance with the sexiest man in the club by far, yet it never was enough for you." Moira intervened.

Dahlia immediately jumped to her own defense. *"I left because I refused to be stripped from my womanhood. Ardan would have never allowed this. He would not stand for the way things have been going on here..."* She looked around. *"And I know it has been for quite some time. Looks like they have brainwashed you too, into believing you're invincible. You're not!"*

"You come at me with the emptiness of your sorrows, yet I feel you were rather ungrateful and spoiled. Was Chad not enough for you when your daddy played "house" a little too seriously when you were just a little girl?" She poked out her bottom lip. *"How tragic...and pitiful that must've been?"*

Dahlia stood flustered and abashed. *"You fucking cunt..."*

"Ask Chad how many times he let me suck him off because pretty little Dahlia was too prude to give it up... she was too afraid—fragile with a stained soul. But, what nobody knew was your fear from your father...the first man to ever truly touch you." She gave a subtle giggle.

"Why don't you tell everyone how you made him stop? With a knife above his chest while he slept... lying completely defenseless!" Her voice rose.

"Stop it!" Dahlia begged.

I could tell Moira was getting her rocks off. *"Dahlia knew the only way she could get her way was to make him stop! The only way she could know for certain and what did you do, Dahlia?"* She laughed. *"She killed the man!"*

"Shut the fuck up, you evil bitch! I did what I had to, to protect myself! He was sick...he needed help!"

"So you put that deranged man out of his misery...seems as if little miss Dahlia isn't as perfect as she seems." Moira smiled devilishly.

Cutting her eyes sharp enough to slice through glass, Dahlia crinkled her nose viciously. *"If I remember correctly, you did want to be like me...or perhaps even be me? Do you not remember the day I found you pathetically masturbating after eavesdropping in on me and Chad fucking behind the clubhouse? How you'd drool over the site of him entering the room. I knew you had it out for him, you were happy that I had finally left. I hope you enjoyed having his cock in your filthy mouth as opposed to suffering his strong hands across your delicate face and tiny throat every time he had too much to drink!"* Dahlia looked right at Chad. *"Isn't that right, baby?"* She began walking towards him and I could see his breathing quicken. *"You loved having your hands on me…no matter for what purpose. I swear if it weren't for the passionate sex that had me completely blinded, you would've been the next one on my fucking hit list."* With disturbed rage, Dahlia changed direction and ran at Moira; slamming her to the ground for a brutal fight. Everyone had given the female smack down their entire attention, leaving a perfect window for Draper to run over and cut me loose.

"This was all your fucking plan?"

"Not exactly, but it still worked out in your favor."

Raising his Berretta fearlessly into the air, Draper fired off several rounds to gain everyone's attention. *"Listen the fuck up, I know most of you are tired of how things have turned out. It is no longer about brotherhood, good times and long rides. It's about the lust for power, the thirst for wealth. The greed against what is not earned, but what is taken. This man…"* He pointed towards me. *"He was not given the choice to be here, but in that time he had a vision that things would change for the better. The Old Testament or not, bylaws are fucking bylaws. Why have equal rights when you are being controlled and manipulated by those who poison and take credit for the very things you've worked for?"*

"Because…" I replied. *"Every group needs its leader."* I rose to my feet squeezing off Adam's pistol, placing a deserving bullet into our enemies one by one.

*Click…*Ryder.

Click…Benjamin.

Click…Chad.

Click…Quaestor.

Click…clip was empty.

Panting and doused with mercy, I stood in the middle of a balanced scale and not a single person objected or dared to challenge me and the Army I created to infiltrate one of the baddest motorcycle clubs in our nation.

Something that takes most undercover officers…years; I did in weeks. –Fate.

Epilogue

Two months later...

Sitting at a stoplight, with a brand new flat black Night Train shaking between my thighs, I glanced in the rearview at my fully-patched cut. Wearing a title that held the highest position every member gave the approval for me to display. I beamed with pride feeling the freshly polished nails cut to a point, digging pressure into my ribs. Susurri had her hair pinned up neatly in a bun, wearing a memorial shirt for Adam. To my right, I smiled at my best mate and the Disciples' new V.P.

His face remained emotionless with an unkempt shadow comforting his jawline. The power of women as a whole, clutched to his sides as Dahlia sported a matching shirt.

The flags flailing in the wind attached to Kian's bike made my heart swell, even though Moira who refused to smile my way, gave a side smirk as I turned around to give the lines a glance. Motors ticking and exhaust burning through the fibers of our jeans, a flock of black crows swooped down, soaring through our feet and between each bike.

The light turned green and the new age, newborn and revived Keltic Disciples roared down the highway in a sympathetic formation for an unforgettable member, friend and brother.

Walking down a row of vendors, I made it a point to stop at our club's beer booth. Our newest prospects, Killian and Eamon straightened their posture as we approached. Without having to ask, the young men popped open two bottles of beer, offering them in our direction.

With an offensive tone, Draper took one hand to the bottle and the other to Eamon's cut. The kid's eyes enlarged as his Adam's apple plunged in his throat. *"What about the ladies?"* Draper motioned towards Dahlia and Susurri behind us.

Cocking his head to the side, Draper pulled his

cheeks back into an apologetic smile only to laugh at his own sarcasm as we walked off to join the rest of the festivities Montana had to offer.

"You nearly made that boy piss himself."

"I've learned from the best." Draper winked.

I couldn't help but laugh at the 'Doc' patch sewn in as his nametape.

Even though I couldn't end the war in Afghanistan and I couldn't control the things that have happened. I at least took pride in knowing I made a courageous difference in these people's lives, reminding them of their original history and purpose. I have become a part of something I never dreamed of in a million years, but I also gained an honest understanding of how these individuals work.

I looked to see a patrol car with a former high school buddy wearing a campaign hat above reflective aviators. He recognized me, but gave a subtle nod of respect as we crossed paths. Although I may have done something good to some, I am still labeled as a bad influence and stereotyped as a lawless bastard. Well, that may be so. All the validation and reassurance I needed comes from these men and women I now shared my life with, who I have grown to love through our differences and trials. If we have one thing in common, it's the two wheels we ride on. Let us not forget our previous leader's and take them as a lesson learned and a war well won to becoming stronger than we were during our birth year of 1939. I and my lifestyle may be

frowned upon, but I am just a man like any other—
trying to make it and longing to survive.

Ride Out.

Translation

: Latin to English

Semper Fidelis –Always Faithful

Nequam- Worthless

Abeamus- Let's go

Heus, Perfide- Ouch, you bastard

Et Induxi Vos Aliquid- I brought you something

Genus familia est, sanguinis est sanguis- Family is family, blood is blood

Loqui, pungas- Speak, you prick

Obseres palatum- Shut your mouth

Dominus- Master

Satis fratres- Enough brothers

Intelligi- Understood

Heus, te nequam irrumabo- Hey, you worthless fuck

Quod Satis! - That's enough!

Susurri- Whisper

Nequam pungunt- You prick

Fortunatos- Good luck

Quam Bella? - How attractive?

Nere eum esse hominem, amabo- Sew this on for him, please?

Non omittere- Don't mention it

Gratias- Thanks

Lupatriae filius- Son of a bitch

Prohibere- Stop

Te vita mea- I have your life

Et huc venerunt- Come here

Et amplexatur sustinere- Endure and embrace

Quaeram te, ut non! - Don't make me ask you again!

Nunc! – Now!

Ignavus- Coward

Tu tamen nihil scire- You still know nothing.

Probare gloriantur- Prove boast.

Tu misselus- You're pathetic

Vilis- Fuck you!

Ut mihi tu- Let me have you

Irrumabo- Fuck

Paenitet- Sorry

Id malique fati- Goddamn it.

Teneat eam- Hold it

Sic? - Yes?

Claudere in FUTUO sunt. – Shut the fuck up.

Voluptatem- pleasure

Incumbam- Bend over

Step propius- Step closer.

Gravissimos, potest de defendere-The prick can defend
himself.

Ide- name for "thirst"

Medb- name for "woman who makes men drunk"

Scortum- Whore

Amara- Bitter

O, te ipsum- Oh, go fuck yourself.

Numquam quererrentur- You never complained

Alius, dominus- another, master

Mortem- Death

Audeo tibi- I dare you

Justa loquar ad te- Let me take you away

Dampnas- damn it

Quid hoc malorum est? - What's wrong?

Mouere ualet*!- Move!*

Sic, ubi prospectu- thus, the prospect?

Ut et confunde eos, sed potens est in gullas- He may be
stubborn, but his cock is mighty.

Te fututam eum? - Did you fuck him?

Non, futui me. - No, he fucked me.

Quid futuo? - What the fuck?

Dominus fortis- mighty master

Officium, nunc! - Office, now!

Proditor- Traitor

Egregium opus, Moira- Excellent job, Moira

Pudeat te. - Shame on you.

Mitescere, Benjamin. – Calm down, Benjamin.

Innoxius- He's harmless.

Maxime- By all means.

Semper- Always.

Meretricum- Whores